SEER

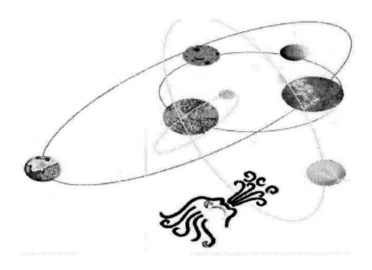

Barbara Paul-Emile

Sunstar
PUBLISHING LTD.

Seer
Barbara Paul-Emile

United States Copyright, 2003
Sunstar Publishing
P.O. Box 2211
Fairfield, Iowa 52556

LCCN : 2003110589

ISBN: 1887472320

Readers interested in obtaining further information on the subject matter of this book are invited to correspond with The Secretary, Sunstar Publishing P.O. Box 2211, Fairfield, Iowa 52556

Dedication

*In appreciation of their loving support,
I dedicate this book to my family:
Serge, Kimani and Erin, Serge Jr.
and the matriarchs,
Moddie and Louisine.*

Acknowledgments

I wish to express my gratitude to my husband, Serge, for his continual loving support and encouragement in the writing of this novel. His unwavering faith in the endeavor was a constant source of strength and inspiration for me. For their helpful advice on all aspects of the project including the reviewing of book covers, I want to thank my daughter Kimani and her husband Erin.

I wish to acknowledge Tony Lanza for his insightful comments on early drafts of the manuscript and Tony Ellis, my editor, for his trouble-shooting skills; in particular, his helpful ideas on how to identify, isolate and present the visionary material in SEER. Shirlee Brockelman's careful reading of the text was a labor of love.

I wish to thank Paule Marshall for her encouragement, her generosity of spirit and her willingness to reach out and assist others. Lastly, I must express my profound thanks to Rodney Charles, my publisher, for his vision, his largeness of soul and his commitment to lighting the paths of others.

Contents

Prologue

$\mathscr{B}$ecka untied her scarf and laid her walking stick beside her as she took her seat in Mirri's large living room. The house had been closed all morning and traces of breakfast: fried plantains and salt fish hung heavy in the air. The elderly woman's walk to the house had been strenuous. The hills seemed higher than ever and the distances longer. She sat for a moment to catch her breath.

Edna, Mirri's neighbor had seen her coming up the hill and had let her into the house with great deference and fanfare, making appropriate apologies for Mirri's absence. Mirri, Edna said, had been called to the Post Office to pick up a parcel. Becka knew that the Post Mistress' hours were erratic at best, and so she seated herself comfortably in Mirri's best chair to await her return. Mother Becka didn't mind the delay. The walk had drained her and she needed some time to rest, to close her eyes and collect her thoughts.

After a time, Becka opened a window and looked out at Mirri's vegetable garden as scents of fresh mint and thyme drifted into the room to clear the stale air. Then she turned to examine her surroundings. Mirri hadn't made many changes. The heavy bureau and large dining table her husband Sojey had made, along with the chest of drawers, were brightly polished and still in use. Mirri was a good housekeeper, but housekeeping and furniture did not hold Becka's attention. She looked at the small room in the corner screened off by curtains.

Mother Becka remembered that evening many years ago when she'd come to Mirri's call. She remembered the fear, the underlying grief that saturated the house that night. She recalled the pain, the anxiety and the sense of deep stillness that sat in the house like a leaden weight. She saw the child, Joe-Joe, lying in the small bed: his life-force waning as he hung between life and death. The weary mother, distraught, afraid, had nowhere to turn.

Becka rose and walked into what had been Joe-Joe's room, now partially a storage space. For all the piled boxes and stacked brown bags, the room looked essentially the same. As she glanced at the scattered objects lying on the floor, Becka remembered how she had concentrated her powers and called on divine aid to cross the bridge between dimensions to bring Joe-Joe back to this earth. Scenes from the night spent in that room came back to her, for they were indelible imprints stamped on her mind.

The child's spirit had resisted returning. Traveling the dimensions had been a perilous journey, a trip to an unforeseeable destination. She had been thrown into galaxies of sound, light and images that dazzled her imagination. She had crossed distortions of time and space to meet multidimensional characters whose every existence destroyed her concept of time and reality.

That night's experience had changed Becka's life. She now knew more about earth-living and the dimensions beyond physical sight than she dared to say. As a shaman, linear time and conventional reality had ceased to matter as she came to understand soul-body and personal relationships in ways never revealed before. Word of her powers had spread and demand for her services grown. Now, she had very little time to herself. This trip to see Mirri was in itself a gift.

Entering the kitchen, Mother Becka made herself a cup of hot mint tea. Sipping the liquid slowly, she returned to her seat and thought of the events that had led to that fateful evening.

Chapter One

The Call

$\mathcal{M}$irri walked across the large room that served as the living area of her house and lifted the curtain that screened off the small room in which her son, Joe-Joe, lay still in his bed. She inhaled sharply, stared at the child and abruptly looked away. She knew that things were not going well. The child was not responding to the medication that the nurse had left. He appeared to be in a deep sleep and seldom moved. His fever had not abated. She had sponged his forehead and tried to feed him a thin broth. All to no avail. Nothing passed between his lips. She had seen little movement and no improvement in three days. Her hands trembled as she adjusted his crisp bed sheets, which reflected the geometric patterns formed by the light of the sinking sun. Mirri took a hold of herself and tried to formulate her thoughts. What was she to do?

Edna, her neighbor and friend, had come to

visit every chance she got and had brought over some of her own medicines in the hope of a cure. Mirri had taken them all hoping that maybe one would work. She had rubbed down Joe-Joe with different ointments and propped him up on pillows to feed him herbal teas. She had prayed and repeated the psalms of King David but nothing had worked. Nothing had worked. Panic began to rise in her throat. Her husband, Sojey, was away from home on business. Her own family lived far away. She felt alone. What was she to do?

Leaving Joe-Joe's room, Mirri walked back into the living room, tugging compulsively at her apron. She closed her eyes and repeated to herself: "I cannot lose my child. God Almighty, help me. I cannot lose my child." Beads of sweat formed on her forehead and the furniture swam before her glazed eyes as does the steaming pavement on a hot day. What was she to do? She must send for help. She must send for Mother Becka.

She walked to the back door of her house and called Edna asking her to send over her son Samuel to run an errand for her. The boy came at once. He was a scrawny, wiry, child, agile, quick, eager and willing to be of service to Mirri. He was Joe-Joe's best friend.

There he stood before the anxious woman, his childish face tight with worry, waiting her command.

Mirri looked at him without really seeing him: "Samuel, go and fetch Mother Becka. Tell her to come quick. Don't come back without her. You hear me, boy. Now go."

She had no smiles for Samuel today, no baked biscuits or sugar-plums; but the boy knew why and shared her fears. Nodding in agreement, Samuel darted off down the road at a sprint, hoping to assure Mirri that he would be quick.

The pace of the sprint was too fast for him to maintain, so Samuel slowed to a jog before reaching the crossroads, again accelerating to a fast trot at the large flamboyant tree, the halfway point of his journey. At first, he felt his strength ebb, but it returned as he built up speed and again broke into a sprint. Keeping his movements fluid, and his breathing even, he focused his mind on reaching Mother Becka's house in the shortest possible time. The sound of his sandaled feet pounding on the stones in the road created a rhythm that helped still his fears and quiet his mind. On his journey, he passed all the familiar sights with which he had grown up but, today, saw nothing. Nothing at all. Houses, animals, people were a blur and he acknowledged nothing and no one, so set was he upon reaching his destination.

Chapter Two

Rêverie

*M*other Becka sat by her favorite stone in the yard. Her blue chambray dress falling between her thin, spaced legs, lightly touching the grass. She stared vacantly into the distance and gently closed her eyes. The day was slowly drawing to a close promising a red sunset and a long twilight. During these magical hours, Becka felt her physical reality begin to thin and give way to dreamtime. Late-blooming flowers released sweet, pungent scents to the evening and the heat of the day retreated before the coming of the cooling breeze.

To Becka, this time between waking and sleeping, when nature slows its pace and the Great Mother rests, was precious and sacred. For a short space, the corners of the etheric dimensions seemed to touch and the curtain that separated worlds dissolved and became less opaque.

Becka recalled her mother saying that in olden

Barbara Paul-Emile

times, the spirits of the ancestors and their companions, the little fairy people, concealed by the shadows of the half-light, would often visit and allow themselves to be seen. Becka thought that she had caught glimpses of them but could never be quite sure. Turning her thoughts into words and mouthing them, the seer said to herself, "Come back among us, gentle ones, come again. We're but foolish humans. Dance for us."

The seer glanced about her yard thinking that the mangoes were particularly big and luscious this year. The devas, nature spirits, had done their work well. The plums, sweetsops, soursops, ripe bananas and star-apples red, green, yellow, tawny, proudly displayed themselves on branches that hang low to the ground. She took a roll of tobacco from her pocket and absent-mindedly pressed a wad into her clay pipe. We should be grateful for all that is given, she thought, and sent out a silent song of thanks to the spirits and the sylphs.

Becka recalled Mother Moro's admonition to her as they walked home from Becka's ritual confirmation at the Pocomania ceremonies.

"Becky, girl," her mother had said, slowing her pace for effect, "you are entering the age of training for spirit-work. Always remember that the real world is inward, child, and not outward. Whereas the outward eye will deceive you, the inner eye never will. Remember that."

She had paused to break off a piece of fragrant

lilac bush.

"Now, daughter, hear me," she had continued, pressing Becka's hand, "you must honor the sight given to you inside more than the sight given outside. Regardless of what the world says; this you must do." Becka had kept scuffing up the trail.

"Do you hear me, girl?" Moro insisted, as she peered intently at Becky as though burrowing deep into her soul.

Becky, shy, had finally murmured her assent.

Her mother had looked down the distant trail ahead and added: "It is the inner truth you must always follow as you take the path of the journey-woman. The way to find it is to listen inward. Take time to listen inward, my daughter."

Becka had nodded her head in agreement, overwhelmed by the moment and intimidated by the wide-reaching implication of her mother's words.

Becka's mother, known to many as Moro, the Wise One, was a loving but strict and principled woman. She had established a school for the village children many years ago. To the young children, she taught reading, writing and arithmetic. To her own daughter, she taught all these subjects, plus the ancient art of divination and other things besides. Moro taught Becka the ways of nature and the wood spirits, the meaning of dreams and the malleable and diaphanous nature of reality. She taught her daughter the healing properties of plants and explained the correlation of the shape of leaves to organs of the body they served. In

Barbara Paul-Emile

short, Mother Moro taught Becka to be a shaman and bequeathed to her sacred books, chants and totems for continued growth.

Becka recalled walking high up in the woodlands, searching for healing herbs with her mother. Sometimes Becka was almost sure that they glimpsed the dazzling shapes of the wood spirits as they darted among the trees, the dappled sunshine catching their reflection and the dark shadows reflecting their fleeting forms. Becka would laugh at their antics as she savored the confirmation that happiness, love and playfulness were the essence of their being. But she never knew whether these images came from inside her own consciousness and were projected outward or vice versa. She just could never tell. All she knew for sure was that she and her mother saw what others did not.

Becka absorbed the fragrant smells and scents of the evening, breathing deeply, then lit the pipe held loosely in her veined hand. These moments between the fading of the harsh light of day and the coming of the soft darkness of night always drew her into an altered state of consciousness. This was her private time when she took her ease and began her retreat from the physical world and third dimensionality. Becka, ever sensitive to the subtle energies around her, responded to the vibration of the evening by relaxing her body and letting her consciousness run free.

As was her custom, Becka tuned in to the psychic net that connected her to the source and visions of the future: things to come, began to flow to her. Suddenly, she had a premonition that she would not have much time to enjoy her rêverie. The messages were insistent. There would be work for her to do tonight. All the signs confirmed this: the sensation in the seventh chakra, the pulsing of the third eye in the center of her forehead, the ominous cries of the sky-hawks overhead, and the feeling of inevitability that accompanied this gift of awareness. The call was coming and she was being forewarned. Further, Becka felt the urgency with which the message imprinted itself on her emotional body.

No additional guidance was given her. Still, the seer kept her inner balance and with an act of will controlled her vibrational levels. There was still some private time left to her. She need not run to meet the future. It was coming to her.

Becka sighed as the languor of the moment freed the spirit from her body. She remembered one of Moro's chants:

> *Surround me with your light this day*
> *That I might feel your blessing*
> *Fill me with your light this day*
> *That I might feel your grace.*
>
> *Be my guide, my friend, my companion*
> *That I might not lose my way*
> *Be with me now*
> *I live within your sway.*

Barbara Paul-Emile

The shaman puffed meditatively on her pipe and allowed the stillness of the evening to permeate her being. For a moment, silence lay in the air like a shimmering jewel refracting the rays of the evening sun.

Chapter Three

The Response

$\mathcal{B}$ecka remained in a light trance that dimmed her physical awareness but honed her psychic sensibilities. The shaman felt her spirit move out of her body and felt the quick, popping sound that told her she was free. She heard the whooshing inner sound that carried her airborne into a galaxy of harmonic sounds and colors:

> *Moving between worlds*
> *Floating, drifting, gliding*
> *Stream-currents, glowing, flowing*
> *Light within light*
> *Spiraling, merging, rising*
> *Inviting, deepening, calling ...*

Becka took a quick breath and prepared her consciousness to enter that state that allowed for her full release. But she could not seem to concentrate. Her

Barbara Paul-Emile

summons was getting closer, steadily nearing.

Becka, suddenly, felt her consciousness plummet back into her body. Her senses became alert to the earthly day-to-day mind that monitored her physical body. She listened, audibly tracking the low rustling of dried banana leaves. Becka opened her eyes and gazed off into the distance at the thick grove of fruit trees bordering her property. She was not tense, but focused. Not apprehensive, but aware. Turning her head to the locus of the sound, she caught the soft padding of sandaled feet on the earth. The young boy approaching was not more than nine years old. She recognized him as Samuel, Edna Hawkin's eldest child. Becka heard his breathing and knew that he had been running hard. Now he had only strength enough for a limping, halting walk.

The spiritwalker's eyes scanned him; he appeared anxious and shaken. His clothes were disheveled and the woman could feel the fear within him. Rising quickly to her feet, Becka reached out her hand to steady the boy and said softly, "What is the matter, child?"

The boy stammered, shifted from one leg to the other as children do, struggling to gain control of himself.

Finally, he got out "Miss Becka, Ma'am, you must come quick. Joe-Joe take sick, him worse. Nurse say she do all she can do. So Miss Mirri send for you." Becka knew of Joe-Joe's illness but had received no summons until now. She recalled her premonitions and realized that this was the message that had appeared in her visions - the journey she had foreseen in her rêverie. Looking back on her activities, she now understood that her guide-spirits had been preparing her for this summons all day.

Just that morning, she had felt the urge to pick fresh herbs and to collect those in the trough, which she had left to dry in the sun. Smiling tolerantly and chuckling to herself, Becka addressed her guides, "You tell me some things, but never everything. Yet, you prepare me well for my task." She gave out a long, low laugh.

Samuel watched her in surprise. To whom was she speaking and why did she laugh? He was puzzled by her benign expression. Maybe she had not heard his words. As though she read his thoughts, Becka shook out her dress, smiled at the boy, patted his head reassuringly and walked to the house with slow, deliberate steps. Becka bowed her head and began to hum silently to herself one of her ritual Pocomania power songs:

> *Steady, steady as we go*
> *Holding on to what we know*
> *Power wash me, power guide me*
> *Lord, sweet Lord, take me ...*

Becka was willing to answer Mirri's call but she needed to know more about the task ahead. In response to her internal query, she was allowed a glimpse of the sick child lying in his narrow bed, his bed sheets unruffled. Becka saw his mother, sitting stiff and dry-eyed by his bedside, keeping anxious watch over her child and awaiting the seer's arrival. Becka kept the scene on her internal view-scan for a few seconds and, shaking her head, realized that the child wanted to leave this world.

On reaching the steps of her small three-room house, the shaman paused and called back to little Sam who was still standing where she'd left him, telling him to fetch the walking stick, which leaned against the kitchen door. The stick had become her friend and, in truth, was needed more for companionship than for support. The boy ran off on his errand as Becka disappeared into the house.

Clutching the stick tightly in his hand, Sam waited impatiently for the seer to emerge from her house. His mind was racing. Miss Mirri, Joe-Joe's mother, had looked so frightened, so worried. He had known her all of his life but had never seen her so nervous, so confused, so afraid. He had not been allowed to see his best friend for several days now. The district nurse had visited Joe-Joe's house all week. Why? What was so wrong? All Joe-Joe had was the flu, a regular cold. His own mother, Miss Edna, had said so.

Mr. Foley, Joe-Joe's father, was away in the neighboring parish of St. Ann, buying provisions for resale at the market. He wouldn't be back until later that week. Miss Mirri was by herself, for her family lived high in the mountains and was not of this parish. She would have to get word to them by the postal van. Again, the vision of the sweat on Miss Mirri's forehead and the marked evidence of fear in the way she twisted her apron and tugged at her headscarf came into Sam's mind. He was afraid to contemplate what might be wrong.

The boy paced back and forth, hitting Becka's stick on the ground. The tight, yellow overall his mother had made for him that he had begun to outgrow, began to chafe, feeling tighter by the minute.

"And where was Miss Becka?" he said to himself. "Why won't she hurry up?" He squinted his eyes against the rays of the dying sun and tried to focus on the entrance to her house.

Samuel had always liked Mother Becka, as the villagers called her, even though he had heard many speak her name in hushed voices saying that she was an obeah woman, a witch woman with powers. The villagers believed that Becka knew about things before they happened. Indeed, many feared that she could make them happen.

People treated Becka with respect, for she was one woman they did not bother or offend in any way for fear of angering her. The villagers sensed that she could cause terrible trouble if so inclined. Yet, it was also known that Mother Becka only helped people. No one had ever claimed to be harmed by her in any way. She healed the sick more often than not, and tended the dying. She counseled the healthy and the living. Yet,

Barbara Paul-Emile

people still talked. People still talked.

With these thoughts racing through his head, Sam found that he was unable to restrain himself any longer and getting up from the large stone on which he sat, he approached Becka's door summoning the courage to knock.

As though on cue, Becka appeared. She had not changed her blue dress but had tied her head with a scarf of the same color. Her boots appeared to be more sturdy, and her bag was full of ointments in addition to her herbs. She smiled her thanks at the boy for his patience and motioned him to exchange her bag for the stick. The transaction completed, both set off for the half-mile walk to Miriam Foley's house.

Chapter Four

The Journey

$\mathcal{S}$am said little to Becka during their walk together, even though the seer invited conversation by asking him about school, his mother, his father and his friends. With each step, the silence between them lengthened. Sam walked at a pace that would accommodate Becka's stride, from time to time checking her face for signs of fatigue. He allowed her to rest her hand on his shoulder whenever they reached a rough stretch of road, but said nothing because he did not feel like talking. His mother always told him when you have nothing to say, say nothing. Recalling this admonition, he remained silent. The woman walking beside him understood his feelings and left him to himself. She had attended his mother at his birth and had watched him grow. Becka knew his nature. He was of a kind and generous disposition, but tended to be reserved, shy and private in his ways.

Becka allowed the child his private time and

became lost in her own rêverie. As they walked along, the shaman could not help realizing how much times had changed. On several occasions, she had to stand and wait at the side of the road for the traffic to go by. The village had grown in many ways: some positive, others not so positive. People had become so busy now. She could not help remembering the old days. She smiled to herself and slowly her face softened with sadness.

This is not a time that is good for the world of spirit, she thought. Life has become too hard. People seek only to survive, to feed their families, to punish their enemies and to lose themselves in foolish pleasures. Even the traditional ceremonies and dances, that transported the soul and kept body and spirit alive during the difficult years, were giving way now to the lure of the cinemas and to the bright lights and tin music of the nightclubs in town.

She thought of her cousins, Oonie and Margaret, who after working in the garden and cooking all day, had dressed and gone out for the evening with friends. They said they went to have fun. What was "fun"? Becka thought. That was a new word that had come in with the Americans. The English had never spoken of fun. They knew nothing about it, she was sure, and neither did she.

Ceremonial and communal dancing, these she understood. In olden days, men and women danced as one with the spirits until dawn. They were never tired. Their strength increased as they astral traveled together in dance with the benevolent ones. On the wings of joy and desire, enveloped by the energy of the Great Spirit, they rose into the higher planes and moved as one before their maker. There the dancers, having left this realm, experienced real ecstasy. Becka saw visions of herself with skirt tied high, as she surrendered to the sounds that pierced her soul and took her on that inner journey.

But "fun." What was "fun"? How can one have it? Becka dismissed these thoughts with disdain, pursed her lips, and closed her eyes. She breathed deeply of the scent of sweet lilacs and fever grass that flowed like a wave over her body.

Still, on certain evenings, at twilight, the drums could be heard in the hills. Duncan, a *pocoman*, a leader of the Pocomania sect, held his ceremonies and the faithful still came. Absentees said that there was the land to be tilled and the animals to be cared for, children to be raised and sent to school. They had no time to share with the community or with spirit. Regretfully, Becka acknowledged, with a shrug of her shoulders, that the material world had overtaken the spiritual. Tradition was slipping away and the bonds of communal life were loosening.

Looking at the furrowed field and scrubby gardens, the shaman smiled ruefully to herself. In past years, the villagers had worked harder than they do now, and the ones before them, their slave ancestors, saw no end to work. Labor ate them as they now ate roast breadfruit. No part was salvaged for the seed to nourish new life. Yet the old ones knew how to re-seed themselves. They knew how to nourish the inner force. They did not abandon tradition. They had time to assemble and honor the unseen world that supports the seen. They knew how to use the little space given them by their masters to replenish themselves. Pocomania, that is what gave sustenance to their lives: the drums, the dancing and the circle singing of Poco songs.

Times had changed, indeed, and the people's vision was earth-bound. They had no time for the old ways, or for old memories. Yet, when faced with the trials and tribulations of life, they turned to spirit and to Becka. When the doctors and the upper-class ministers, in whom they placed their trust, said there was no hope, no help, "dem ban' dem belly" and came to her. They came to Becka. Some came in secret and by night, tapping softly at her door and window. Others came by day and in the open, walking boldly through her gates. Others sent messengers. The seer always listened to their pained voices, watched their weary faces and offered comfort and solace. She gave them teas, poultices and ointments and guided them to the opening of their own hearts and to the healing powers that lay within. The shaman took no pride or credit for her cures. She knew that her strength and her 'knowing' came from one source, spirit.

When Becka and Samuel reached Low River Turning, they saw approaching a group of workmen returning from the field, singing the latest calypso. Their version of the song was not meant for Becka's ears, for while they kept true to the melody, the lyrics were improvised. The reasons why Mr. James, the Justice of the Peace, had a wife and more than one mistress, had received considerable raunchy embellishments. New lyrics had been added, pointing to the difficulty the Justice had keeping track of numbers. Did he have trouble with addition, subtraction and division, especially division? Did he want to know how many times one can go into three or maybe four? Or did three and one equal two? The singers laughed uproariously at their bawdy puns.

The group lapsed into silence, however, as they passed the matriarch, tipping their caps to her in respect. They made sure that she was out of earshot before they started up again. Becka smiled to herself gently, because she had heard these songs before and knew of the amusing improvisations. She had watched several of the young men grow up and had birthed some. She knew the satisfaction these songs of social defiance, which ridiculed the middle and upper classes, brought them. Calypso was a great equalizer.

Becka walked along in silence, speaking only to well-wishers with whom she shared the usual courtesies. When she and Sam started up Spring Mount Hill, the seer tried once more to engage the young man in conversation. She knew that speaking would ease the child's pain and confusion by allowing him to talk about his fears. This time she asked him about his pet rabbits. In response, not only did Sam tell her about his pets but also about his friendship with Joe-Joe who

Barbara Paul-Emile

helped him on several occasions to chase troublesome rabbits out of his mother's garden. The seer and the boy laughed heartily at the escapades and the strain was somewhat lifted.

Becka kept her hand resting lightly on the lad's shoulder, partly to steady him emotionally and partly to keep up with the increasingly brisk pace he was setting. She listened to the chirping of crickets as dusk descended and the sun sank deeper in the west. She heard the cackling sounds of chickens flying up to roost in trees for the night. She heard mothers calling wayward children home to be washed and fed before nightfall.

As the road wound up Steely Hill, Becka's thoughts turned in on themselves and images from last night's dreamtime drifted into her mind. She remembered the rich, ornate cage in which a silvery mouse had been caught. She had been touched by its helplessness and decided to come to its aid. The little animal had peered out at her through the bars, its tiny eyes dancing furtively back and forth, as she worked mentally at unlocking the cage. Granted its freedom, it had leapt out and scampered off across the floor, but not before turning to acknowledge her kindness. The creature had changed into a beautiful horse running joyously across an open field with the wind in its mane. She had been impressed by its shapeshifting abilities and had wished it well. In dreams all things were possible and nothing was strange.

The seer kept track of her dreams, for, with the

sensitivity of a mystic, she knew that the known rests on the unknown, the light upon the dark, and the conscious upon the unconscious. A couple of nights earlier, she had dreamt that she was walking through a woodland where the trees grew bright silver leaves. On each leaf, she had vaguely discerned a human face. A high-flying bird had hovered above. Faintly, she had heard voices and music as the wind, rustling through the leaves, made a tinkling sound. The scene had been lit by a bluish-white light, and minute crystals, like confetti, had shimmered everywhere. The atmosphere had been eerie and the setting weird and unearthly, yet all had been strangely beautiful in its way. The dream had not made known its meaning to her. All her rational mind could do was gnaw at it. Wisely, she placed it in her dream file, for she knew that all answers would come in their own good time.

Becka and Sam turned at the crossroads onto a small dirt path where houses were grouped together on the side of a hill. Some were brightly painted, others were but rundown shacks. An unplanned line of demarcation separated the dwellings. The painted houses, well kept by their owners, usually had some land attached and carefully tended vegetable gardens. The shacks, unpainted, bare, defiant in their ugliness, stood surrounded by discarded objects and weeds. Window shutters went unfixed, roofs leaked, and naked children ran around untended.

These dwellings were raised up on Mr. Dury's land, where, from time to time, amid much squabbling, bickering and posturing, the belligerent landowner would threaten to get the squatters off with the help of the law. The squatters, unimpressed, would appear with machetes, willing to challenge the law itself in defense of their homes. After the last confrontation, that almost lead to the burning of his downtown office, Dury, a man blessed with common sense, had decided to leave well enough alone and seek other remedies. Becka heard that a deal was being struck whereby the land would be bought by the government and re-sold for a pittance to the residents. Even the authorities knew when to leave well enough alone. As Becka mused about the situation, the scent of fried fish, pepper and onions, roast breadfruit and red bean sauce wafted through the air, mixed with the smell of garbage and stale urine.

All was quiet on this day, as Becka approached Mirri's house which situated on its own plot, painted bright blue and white, and marked by a garden full of large yellow pumpkins, pale green cho-chos and a short sour-sop tree. Miss Mirri, who had been looking out of her window constantly, rushed out to greet the couple. Her face, taut with unshed tears, showed that she was doing all she could to contain her sorrow. Mirri knew that her son was sinking, slipping away. What was she to do?

Little Sam watched, his voice mute. He stood stiff and unmoving as though hypnotized by the mother's grief. The same jagged pain he had felt earlier shot through him as he watched Miss Mirri shudder, cry out and break, tears streaming down her face. He looked away from her, confused and afraid, unable to face her pain. Becka went up to the younger woman, cupped her gaunt dark face between her hands, held her close and comforted her. Mirri wept openly, sobbing, as would a child in its mother's arms. The seer murmured soothing words to her and led her gently into the house.

Chapter Five

The Strengthening

$\mathscr{B}$ecka asked if the sick child's father, Sojey, had been notified of the developing situation. Mirri said she had tried to get word to him. Mother Becka said they should try again and instructed Sam to go to the Square and send word to Sojey by any traveling conveyance going toward St. Ann's Bay. Sojey should be told to return home at once, for his energies would be needed. The boy ran off, eager for something else to do, relieved to know that he could be of further help.

Sam, ever an imaginative child, exaggerated the message to ensure that Sojey understood the dire nature of the emergency.

He asked the side-man on a departing truck to tell Marse Sojey, "Not to stop at any rum-shop tonight and drink up him money with friends. Him must come right home for Miss Mirri and Joe-Joe need him. Joe-Joe sick, bad, bad."

The man assured Sam that Sojey would be told

and sent his respects to Miss Mirri.

The shaman was taken quickly to the bed where the sick child lay in a deep slumber. Gently, she examined him, walked away, and uttered a sigh. She called for more light and threw the windows open. Mirri's house smelled of camphor and of the cirossi bush-bath used to rub down the child. The house was dark and permeated by fear and anxiety; the air was stale and dank.

Becka knew just how important Joe-Joe was to his family. Sojey, an older man, feared that he would have no more children and Mirri, though young looking, had become a mother only after several failed attempts. If this child were to pass from their lives, the suffering would be more than they could bear. Would they be able to overcome it and stay together? Grief translated into pain and pain made people cruel. Tonight, Becka knew she would need all her guides at her side to face the challenges that lay ahead.

The seer had been in this house many times, always in times of joy and happiness when there was every reason to rejoice. The marriage and welcoming of new life were times of celebration. Now, she was here for a more distressing reason: the possible approach of death. In this house tonight, the pain, fear, grief and shock were palpable and the silence ominous.

The shaman slipped off her scarf, yanked off her heavy walking boots and prepared for the work ahead. She called for soap and water to wash her hands, and lemon and rose-water for the ritual rinse.

She called for fresh mint and fever grass for the tea, and strong-back and chainey-root for the bath. She called for scented candles for soft light. She called for spirit's presence, the source and support of life.

Slowly and noiselessly, the obeah woman re-entered the room where the sick child lay. She walked around the bed, moving always to the right, and quietly studied the child even more carefully. He lay absolutely still and seemed hardly to be alive. Joe-Joe appeared very frail, his complexion was ashy and his breath, shallow and slow. Becka took out a small bottle filled with herbs, which she always carried with her, and touched it to his nose. The patient stirred uneasily. The seer questioned the mother more fully about the nature and length of the illness, taking care to give no gesture or sign that would alarm her.

Mirri said that he had come down with what seemed like the common flu a fortnight ago. She had given him the usual remedies, expecting a quick recovery as in the past, but this time it was not so. She had sent for the district nurse and, for a time, he seemed to be getting better, but the cough persisted and now the fever was higher than ever. She feared that the child had no strength left to fight. She saw him slipping away. The big hospital in the city was a day's journey and he had declined so rapidly. Now, the child was too weak to travel.

Mirri, exhausted from her emotional recounting, drew a chair to the table, sat down, and covered her head with her apron. Her shoulders heaved and her whole body shook uncontrollably. At that moment, Edna, Mirri's friend and neighbor and Sam's mother, entered the house and called out a courteous greeting to Becka. On seeing Mirri's weakened condition, her face fell and she ran to where her friend sat and, kneeling, embraced her. The two women hugged each other and rocked back and forth, as though to assuage the all-consuming grief that threatened to overwhelm them.

The shaman, peaceful, centered, appeared oblivious to the drama taking place in front of her. She went to her medicine bag and selected herbs which she calmly gave to Mirri and Edna, along with careful directions on their preparation. One batch should be boiled, steeped and strained into a tea. The other must be boiled along with the strong-back and chainy-root into a brew with which to bathe Joe-Joe's body.

While the women worked together fervently in the kitchen, Becka sponged Joe-Joe's forehead with cool water from Gully Spring, chanting softly to herself. After the bath-brew had been prepared and cooled, and the tea made, Edna wanted to linger but Mother Becka discouraged her for it was time to begin the work. The neighbor returned home to put supper on the table. The seer called for a large bath pan to be brought and, working in silence, Mirri and Becka sponged Joe-Joe's body with tepid, bitter medicinal waters.

Mirri's hand shook as she touched her young son. No, she thought to herself, this cannot be happening. Not my child. Not my child. This boy has been healthy all of his life. Images streamed into her head, breaking her focus showing her child at his usual activities. After Joe-Joe had been washed and dried, both women struggled to get his limp arms into his nightshirt.

Mirri recalled that, up until now, her biggest worry had been how to keep this active child out of mischief. She remembered the day she sent him to Mr. Chen's shop for groceries. On the way home he had placed the grocery bag on the ground in the neighbor's yard to play cricket for a few minutes with his friends. The neighbor's dog had opened up the bag and eaten the ham, the saltfish, the butter, the bread and the patties. The dog had gone through everything, and what he had not eaten he had taken away. How she had yelled at him that day, fed him no supper, and told him that he was a trial to her.

At home, Joe-Joe never sat down. He was forever dragging his old, tired, wooden trucks around the yard, calling out the change of gears from first to second as he charged up imaginary hills. Yet, he was so loving and helpful to her that she could not imagine a better son. Now, he lay still showing little indication of life. Where had his fire and all that energy gone? Where was Joe-Joe's spirit? She feared that he would not see the morning.

The spiritwalker sensed the mother's anxious thoughts. She knew what Mirri feared. Life-energies frequently failed at night or during the early morning hours when the bonds that tie body to spirit were most frail. It was during these times that the human-spirit most frequently departed and the mother was instinctively afraid, sore afraid of the descending darkness. The shaman sensed the downward turn of the woman's energies but gave no sign of what she knew. Her actions were measured and deliberate and by sheer force of her powerful will, she kept Mirri calm. This courageous mother could not be allowed to break and utter the wrenching wail that grieving mothers make when crazed with pain.

Becka glanced at Mirri and noticed the tears streaming down her face. Tears are good, the seer thought. They cleanse the emotions and soften the heart. Grief withheld, on the other hand, bitter mind-numbing grief, saps the strength, weakens the will and breaks the spirit.

Mirri must be made to know that this was a time she needed spirit's strength. She needed its unyielding fortitude, its inner knowing, its subtle promptings, its vigilant guardianship, its protective care and its eternal presence.

Becka remembered the words often used by her mother to calm the broken-hearted. Tonight, they applied to Mirri for she also must reach:

A place within and yet apart
A place where pain does not break the heart
Or hold us hostage to our bitter fears
A place where life is held most dear

Where peace and tenderness abide
A place of life, love, light
Birthright!

Joe-Joe's body hung limp in the hands of the women during the bath. He didn't respond to their ministrations and was oblivious of their presence. Mirri told the shaman that her son had slept all day and had eaten nothing since the night before. Becka wrapped the child in cool sheets and said little, knowing Joe-Joe was in a deep coma. His spirit no longer honored the body by its presence. The body was waiting, waiting on the decision of spirit. This truth the seer would not share with the grieving mother whose conscious mind must be an ally, not an enemy.

After their task was completed, Becka took Mirri gently by the arm and led her to the kitchen where she warmed and sweetened the tea, which had been brewed earlier. The shaman stirred in two teaspoons of liquid from a vial she took from her bag and offered the tea to the weary mother. Mirri sat on the kitchen stool and sipped gratefully. It was her first nourishment of the day.

After Mirri had drained the dark, fragrant liquid, the seer led her to bed and encouraged rest. Becka knew exactly how and where to massage Mirri's body to release the tension, the pent up emotion. She knew exactly what words to say to release the fears lodged deep in the woman's heart. She knew how to get her to let go and to shift the load to spirit.

The shaman was experienced in harnessing Mirri's woman-strength, centering it in her strong, black body.

Becka knew that if her night's work was to be accomplished, the fatigued mother must rest. As she worked on Mirri, a poem learned long ago from Moro's books drifted into the seer's consciousness:

Look away, now, look away
When shadows flow between you
And the light
When rains come and valleys are full
Look away, look away;

When storms increase
And the land is barren
The sun remains stationary
And the moon hangs low and hovers ...
When ley lines coil like serpents
Look away, look away;

When those you love enter the woods without
you
And you fear for their return
When you call for guardianship and protection
Fearful of treacherous terrain
Look away, look away

*For **I am** here.*

Within moments, Mirri began to unwind and

her limbs to slacken as a deep sense of relaxation overcame her. Strong muscular contractions periodically shook her, but gradually the tension drained away and her body became limp.

Before sinking into sleep, however, Mirri summoned up all of her reserves and, holding fast to the seer's arm, raised herself up and murmured, "Mother Becka, in God's name, help my boy. Help little Joe-Joe. He was God's gift to us. Sojey and me need to see him grow into a full man." She fell back on the bed, drowsy and exhausted.

Becka gave her assent and assured her that everything possible would be done. In a soft, soothing voice, the healer told the mother to trust in spirit and know that "God Almighty never shut him eye."

Snatches of the day's activities drifted through Mirri's mind as a languor took hold of her body. With the sound of Becka's hushed voice in her ear, the mother uttered a soft moan and drifted from the cruel rotation of time into the larger expanse of sleep, to a place of healing where pain and the conscious mind dare not follow.

Chapter Six

Nightwatch

$\mathcal{B}$ecka returned to Joe-Joe's room where the boy lay unchanged, silent, a waif in white sheets. He felt warm to the touch, for his fever was high. The spiritwalker drew the drape that separated the boy's room from the main living area and sat on a chair by his bed. The house was still. The evening had given way to nightfall and the neighborhood had quieted down for the night.

Mirri was resting now and would wake restored in the morning. The night belonged to Becka. The shaman studied the frail form lying in the bed and thought of the appropriateness of his pet name, Juppy, which Sojey had given him in infancy. The child seemed so other-worldly, as though the thread that held him to life was thin and badly frayed. A shudder passed through the seer's body as she felt the pain that would wrack the family should the child not recover. There must be a way, the shaman thought, as she turned her crystal talisman over in her hand, to bring this child's spirit fully back into his body. There must be a way to return him to health and to his family. There must be a way.

Becka sat quietly and looked about the small room as though to familiarize herself with it. She saw Joe-Joe's cricket bat and two balls ready for use, wedged in one corner of the room. In another, was the old straw hat Mirri insisted be worn to protect Joe-Joe's hair from turning red in the sun. The child's shirt and pants were hung loosely in a partially completed closet. The rest of his clothing was folded carefully and placed in a make-shift chest of drawers.

The seer blew out the lamp that now burned too brightly on the nightstand, and lit a candle instead. The soft light cloaked the room in shadows. The muffled sounds of night creatures, the fragrance of the frangipani tree and the night-blooming jasmine drifted in through the open window. Sweet cedar gum bark burned in the saucer. The seer looked at the boy's vacant face and began to follow her breath, breathing deeply. Within moments, her consciousness began to shift. Becka knew that the journey she would undertake this night would be a long and arduous one. Breathing even more deeply, she relaxed her body and invited her guide-spirits into the room.

She chanted softly:

Old ones, bright ones
Come among us, once again

Old ones, loving ones
Lift our spirits, our bodies mend.

Draw down and touch this earth
Draw close as at our birth
Old ones, bright ones
Come among us once again.

The physical reality of the room began to shift and to break up and the outline of the bed grew vague and receded from view. Two shining beams of light that grew in intensity as they drew closer came into her line of vision. Becka made out two figures: one male, one female. Their garments were loose and flowing. The female's shimmering clothing was tied at the waist by a wide band, while the male's fell straight and untrammeled to the floor. The halo around their bodies pulsed to a slow rhythm. These luminous beings betrayed no fear or anxiety. They exuded peace, great caring and deep compassion. Becka had met similar entities before and so felt no fear. She understood that they were Joe-Joe's guides and were ever with him.

Her own mother, Moro, had taught her much about the relationship between humans and spiritual entities in preparing her for her work. Becka was quite aware that all humans are accompanied into earth life by two or more guides, whose role it is to love and support and, if needed, nudge them along on their journey. Seen or unseen, the guides are always there. The band of fear that encircles humans is so intense

Barbara Paul-Emile

and restrictive, however, and the sense of separation so strong, that generally it prevents sensing or seeing these bright ones.

Becka was heartened by their presence and felt the energy in the room lift as these intergalactic beings revealed themselves. She knew how to converse with them, for they communicated telepathically, reading thoughts and intentions. Becka watched the halo around their forms glow with a great white light and sent out a question: "Will the spirit of this child return fully to its body?"

The answer came back into her consciousness swiftly: "Joe-Joe is our charge. He is dearly loved and treasured. In this, his ninth year of life on the planet Gaia, he must decide whether he will return to our side of the veil or stay on yours. He has co-created this illness to facilitate his release. Do not fear for him for he is very well. We will protect his body until he has made his decision."

At that moment, the bed and the boy came again into view. Becka heard the child's low breathing and complimented the guides for so ably maintaining the delicate integrity of the body. The atmosphere of the room was charged with feelings of gentle love and tenderness. Becka absorbed the energy, settled herself, and returned to her questions. "Why did Joe-Joe need to make this decision at this time? Where is he now?"

The shaman knew from her experience that these entities would tell her no more than they felt it appropriate for her to know. She must wait and find out what they willed.

Becka's consciousness shifted again and this time Joe-Joe's life appeared before her in a series of audio and video snapshots. She saw him playing cricket with his friends. Heard him shout with laughter as the ball soared into the air. She saw him walking alone into the hills, sitting on a rock and looking out dreamily over the valley with such a sense of longing, as though something or someone he sought was lost. She saw him newly born lying on warm sheets taking his first breath.

Becka saw Joe-Joe dressed in the short pants and shirt his mother made for him, playing truant from school, fishing in a nearby pond. She saw him sitting attentively in school with his classmates, listening to his teacher. The boy had many interests but his favorite subject was geography. The study of this material seemed to mesmerize him. The seer was given to know that the young boy's interest in strange lands expressed his love for the unknown and his willingness to take risks. His longing to travel expressed a need to enlarge his understanding of earth as home.

The spiritwalker shared the child's consciousness as he sat in class and dreamed of the veldts, the grasslands of Southern Africa; the thick forest of the Amazon; the cold and windy, barren high-lands of Russia; the old and magical kingdoms of India; and the fabled lost civilizations of South East Asia. She felt his imagination soar, becoming large and expansive as images took shape and swam in his head.

Becka was overwhelmed by the intensity of the stimuli. She had forgotten how active an imagination a nine-year-old had. The knowledge she had gained of the boy's loves and interests delighted her because she felt that one who so loved nature, and who was so fascinated by human history, would surely be willing to heal himself and live out his life. She thanked his guides for granting this review.

As panoramic landscapes of snow-covered mountains, hot sweltering plains and canopied jungles began to dissolve and disappear, Becka felt her consciousness drawn once again into her own body. Using her internal scanner, the seer sent out a call to Joe-Joe. Again his guides allowed Becka to enter the child's consciousness. This time she was permitted to look out again through his eyes as he examined an atlas on his desk at school. The book had broken open to display the shimmering Caribbean with its string of emerald islands strung like a necklace against a sky-blue sea.

The images seemed to come alive, and Becka could smell the salty scent of the water and hear the calls and cries of the sea birds. She was again impressed by the power of the imagination to conjure up such rich, sensory detail.

As the noises began to drift away and the image to fragment and disintegrate, Becka found herself on a vast green, grassy slope. Below it flowed a slow-moving river. She could hear the splashing of the water over the rocks and saw the sunlight refracted on its surface. The image held her enthralled. She felt herself drawn in by the repetitive undulating current of the water. How long she remained mesmerized, she did not know.

Suddenly, she noticed that a figure had formed itself and was rising up out of the river. It was a dazzling entity on whose form the water shimmered with such intensity as to cause her to look away momentarily. Its clothing was translucent and its face appeared hydrophanous. It exuded such power and confidence that, for a moment, Becka felt confused and was at a loss to interpret what she saw.

The entity was gracious. It waited for her to recover her psychic balance. Becka struggled for control. The scene did not hold steady, it seemed to float in and out of her vision. With effort Becka focused her gaze and finally the scene settled and held. The radiant being remained stationary as though waiting for her to gain control of herself. Remembering the purpose of her mission, the seer asked, telepathically, "Where is Joe-Joe."

Instead of responding immediately, the entity moved closer to her creating a path of light wherever it trod. The magnetic force of the energy it carried was so strong that Becka began to feel that she was being absorbed. Unexpectedly, a powerful light matrix in the center of its forehead pulsed and Becka felt herself infused by a rain of silver lights that surrounded her and disappeared into her auric field. The seer felt her energy rise, her strength increase, and her light-body glow with a new translucency. Her energy stores were being replenished and augmented.

In the presence of this mysterious being, Becka felt empowered. Never in all of her astral travels had she met one of such magnificence, such magnetism, and such power. To be in its energy field was to be enlarged, to be elevated, to be transported to levels beyond anything she had ever known before. She sent out another message of inquiry. "Who are you?" Certainly, he was more than a guide.

The answer came sweeping into her consciousness, "I am the Satron, Light-Keeper. I am many, yet I am one. I manifest as I will and I gather experience for the whole."

In the brief moments that Becka waited before the Satron, she searched her mind and tried to remember all that she had been taught by Moro. Nothing from that mystical curriculum came to mind that could help her now. "What was expected of her?" she wondered. "How should she act in the presence of such an entity?" She had helped people heal them-selves with the assistance of their guides. She had met and conversed with those who had passed on. She had seen and predicted the future, but never had she experienced anything remotely similar to this. "Yes," she said to herself, "this is another experience all together."

Almost imperceptibly, the images before Becka's eyes began to dissolve, first at the edges and, finally, melted away completely. The river, the magnificent being: everything was gone. She watched as new elements began to formulate themselves. The dreamwalker found herself in what appeared to be a rich and sumptuous room with books, manuscripts, scrolls and art objects from ceiling to floor. She had visited the archdeacon's study. She had visited several local libraries, including the famous one in the capital city. She had spent time at Bethel Teachers' College but nothing she had ever seen had prepared her for this. The room was rectangular in shape but from where she stood she could not see its end. The windows were large and airy and overlooked a vast picturesque garden, designed in attractive geometric patterns. The books on the wall were handsomely bound and decorated with richly textured coverings, bright with inlaid jewels. In between the shelves were brightly covered tapestries. Everywhere, there were soft couches, rugs and chairs, so richly upholstered as to surpass anything she had ever imagined. The overall effect was one of luxury and magnificence. Becka felt weak and sank down unceremoniously into one of the nearby chairs.

The seer's light-body, freer and more maneuverable than her physical one, bore no volume or weight, hence no indentation could be seen on the cushion where she sat. Still, she felt herself seated comfortably and continued to survey her surroundings. Astral traveling was not new to Becka. What was new was the meeting of such an impressively dazzling entity and the feeling of anticipation she had that much more was to come.

Barbara Paul-Emile

Chapter Seven

Shapeshifting

$\mathcal{T}$he Satron had reshaped himself and appeared before her now as an older man in casual modern dress. He was slightly gray at the temples and his skin was the shade of dark mahogany. Although he appeared less intimidating and in image more familiar, Becka felt uncomfortable. The Keeper, having taken a seat opposite her, registered the fluctuation in her energy.

He said, telepathically, "Do not be afraid. You are a shaman and a seer: one of the aware ones. You are manifesting in physical form in this century. In your journey to earth, you have elected to have your memory banks erased so that you might experience Gaia in all her forms of light and dark, and help lead those lost in illusion back to the light. You are in your rightful home now and all is well. If you wish to return to your body, you can achieve this by desiring it. You have spiritwalked before. This is different only in that you will be taught so much more. If it comforts you to revisit your body, please do so." He smiled at her as though giving her permission.

Becka thinks of Joe-Joe's room. Immediately, the scene before her begins to fragment and she is in her body, eyes closed in trance, sitting by Joe-Joe's bed. She sees the child's guides, with wings outspread, serene in the conduct of their duty. Her own personal guardians, Anin and Anna, stand behind her body. The house is quiet. Mirri is in deep sleep and Sojey has not yet returned.

Satisfied that all was well, Becka called the Satron and the library back into her mind and the scene was restored.

The Keeper appeared pleased at her return and complimented the seer on her skill in manipulating realities. Becka felt strengthened and supported by the entity's benign presence. To her, he resonated benevolence and peace and she sensed in him a strong desire to impart learning. Cloaked though he was in conventional clothing, the light he carried issued forth from the edges of his form and his aura filled the room. Still, the dreamwalker had no clear idea who the Satron was. His introduction had not satisfied; it had only heightened her curiosity. To carry such light, he must be a being of very low density and high vibrational frequency. His antennae must stretch far into many unknown worlds, the seer surmised.

Becka noticed that he used a kind of inner sound when he communicated with her that was sharper and clearer than anything she had ever heard before. Sometimes, she caught glimpses of designs and shapes that free-floated into her consciousness along with his transmissions. At other times, in his eagerness to speak with her, he directed great chunks of information at her that she had difficulty processing. The shaman knew that she sat before a treasury, a storeroom of knowledge, which she had only to access in order to learn. She felt dizzy from the exhilaration that accompanied this realization.

Almost immediately, the figure of an attractive younger man in formal business suit began to take form. He wore a dark, pin-striped suit, well tailored, expensive white shirt and bright college tie.

The character smiled at her quizzically as though to say, "Did I get this one right?"

Becka shot back, "Yes, except for the shoes."

The young man wore loose sandals such as those worn by the Keeper when he was trying out casual attire. Playfully, the Satron pretended to be devastated by the fashion flaw and immediately manifested shiny black shoes matched by silk socks.

The incredible nature of what was actually taking place shook Becka, and she laughed out loud and with abandon as though she were in the wild hills of her island home. Her laughter filled the room. The sound resonated on the air, was captured and transformed into musical chords that clung to the ceiling as small, silver, oval particles, which then floated gently to the ground.

Becka's sense of the nature of reality had changed drastically, to say the least, since she first met the Satron. Much had happened to make a mockery of what she thought possible or impossible. The Keeper watched her, following her thoughts, obviously pleased by her observations and deductions. He decided to try on several new and different personalities. He shape-shifted into a sun-bronzed warrior, complete with helmet and spear; a mother hanging out her wash in her back yard; a burly farmer with his scythe on his way to the fields; a pimply male adolescent hardly out of puberty, in an old T-shirt and jeans; a stubborn two-year-old girl resolutely refusing to go to sleep; and a Tibetan monk complete with saffron robe.

Becka was dazzled by the display of his shapeshifting abilities. What powers! It was certain that she was no longer in the third dimension where physical reality, because of its density and bulk, held fast its form. Images were light and vaporous and were easily created here. Her bewilderment grew. What did it all mean?

Satron responded to Becka, telepathically, "These talents are all yours. In the third dimension, form is heavy, cumbersome and fixed. You are encased in physical bodies and so your molecular structure is harder to shapeshift, yet not impossible. In the fourth dimension and above, bodies are lighter and less dense and so it is easy. Change is accomplished by using thought and focus. Do not be disheartened, soon you will do it all yourself, traversing dimensions at will."

Finally, the Satron settled on an image with which he felt comfortable. The entity in male form, seated before Becka, had a kindly and intelligent face, much lined by the experience of his years. He wore a nondescript brown suit with a white shirt opened at the neck. The shoes were of the hard leather worn by men in the rural parts of Jamaica and the hands resting lightly on his knees had known rough work. In this image, Becka saw her father, Zeke, who had served as deacon at the Pentecostal church.

Satron, light-being, had taken the image of a father whom Becka dearly loved and she felt her heart opening to him as the seeds of trust were implanted. She felt comforted by memories of family and relaxed even more deeply in the presence of this mysterious entity.

Immediately, memories of past relationships came flooding back to Becka. Her father had been much liked but he did not fit well into the life of the district. He was not a successful farmer, even though he had worked hard all his life. His land never produced to expectations. It was often his wife, in her role as midwife and healer, who provided for the family. Mother Moro never complained. She accepted and loved this man as he was and taught her daughter to do the same.

If times had been different, Zeke probably

would have been a writer or a painter, for he was highly intelligent, sensitive and creative. In his environment such career paths were not options. Hence, he farmed badly, read widely, drew pictures of community scenes, and often sat with his back against a tree, lost in his own world.

Zeke had encouraged his daughter to become an elementary or secondary school teacher. He was joyous when, after high school, she was awarded a scholarship to Mandeville Teachers' Training College for he had hoped to see her safely established in the professional class. But that was not to be, for Becka had her own mind. Although she did very well academically, and completed her course, she had no wish to be confined to dingy classrooms and to the arbitrary dictates of the Department of Education. Responsive to the world of spirit, she loved the freedom of the outdoors and elected, rather, to follow her mother's calling. Moro's teaching had taken a deep and abiding hold on her psyche and on her imagination, that teachers' training classes could not touch. Zeke did not attempt to change his daughter's mind, for he knew it would be useless to try. Furthermore, he loved her independent spirit.

Becka was discovering that maintaining form in the high intensity of the entity's vibrational field was difficult. The power of his emissions was causing her energies to fade and the lights of her own auric field to dim. Immediately, the Keeper sensing her distress and vulnerability, showered her dream-body with shimmering light pellets as he had done before.

The angelic being smiled and directed the spiritwalker to look at herself.

Becka realizes that she has regressed in age and is now a young woman. Gone are the heavily veined and wrinkled hands. Her skin, supple and soft, is the color of a moonless night. She marvels at having her youth restored. She notices that she is wearing one of her favorite dresses: drop-waisted, red floral, with matching headband. She hears the chatter of her friends as they walk with her to the neighborhood curry-goat picnic. She hears the drums and the music of the fife in the distance, as they run to the district fair, fearful of being late. Becka thinks that, for a moment, she sees her mother's face as she appeared when scolding her daughter for having neglected a duty.

The seer moved her thoughts away from her changed form and began a telepathic conversation with the light-being.

"I have come to find Joe-Joe's spirit," she said. "His parents long for him. Their pain will be too great to bear if they lose him. Please help me find this boy's spirit and get him to return. He barely rests in his body now, for his essence is no longer there."

Becka hoped that in his response, the entity would not only be of assistance in her search, but would tell more about himself and why he had chosen to meet her.

In response, Satron, Light-Keeper, pulsed his aura and rose to his feet. He continued to communicate with Becka through thought-transference carried on inner sounds, embellished with swift flowing imagery. At first, it was difficult for the seer to focus her consciousness in such a way as to track the sounds while monitoring the flashes of images. Her efforts brought on feelings of fatigue and again the Keeper's crystalline pellets restored her.

Aware of her dilemma, the Satron transmitted, "To hold your focus, you must banish fear, you must believe that this is possible."

Becka tried to let go of the anxiety and allow a deep sense of "knowing" to move into her being. She felt like a tightrope walker trying to maintain balance while walking at great heights. At any moment, she could lose her footing. She tried to follow the Satron's lead, to trust in her innate abilities.

Gradually, the seer began to feel empowered. She felt as though a new and unfamiliar consciousness flooded her dream-body. It was as though she was switched on. Suddenly, she felt much more centered and focused. So powerful was the surge of the current that raced through her light-body, that she felt sure that she could now maintain her integrity. The entity watched her and registered pleasure and satisfaction with her progress.

He continued: "I am a Keeper of light-entities. I am Joe-Joe, yet I am much, much more. The boy you

Barbara Paul-Emile

seek is within my essence and is but one manifestation of myself. We are intimately connected. We are one. You must know, also, that this entity you seek has the right to choose the dimension in which he exists. He is free to create his own reality."

Becka felt the authority and the beneficence of the speaker. She was at once impressed and confused by his startling pronouncements. "How can he be Joe-Joe?" she thought. "How can he be Joe-Joe and yet more?"

Images of a log rolling down a steep hill began to form in her mind. Mentally, she moved to stop them, to slow the speed, to somehow restore pacing. She was not succeeding and the images vanished as quickly as they had appeared.

Calmly and patiently, the Satron allowed impressions and fragments of thoughts to coalesce in the dreamwalker's mind. He was aware that Becka's perceptions, conditioned by the limitation of third density, offered no answers to her questions.

"Form your questions. Be patient with your-self," the Keeper continued. "What would you like to know?"

As new thought patterns grew and took shape, the seer felt her mental processes expand to accommodate added information. She could feel higher levels of cognition being implanted in her consciousness.

The shaman's sense of the nature of reality was beginning to expand. She knew herself to be Becka, but at the same time she felt that she was also more.

Indeed, she felt, inexplicably, that there were many versions of Becka.

"Do I understand what all this means?" she wondered.

The light around the Keeper pulsed and Becka knew the source of her increased awareness. It was as though the door to a storeroom of knowledge had been opened. A flood of rich and varied thought-streams began pouring into her expanded awareness. New words, concepts, paradigms, images, all swam through her cognitive centers. It was as though her consciousness had been amplified. Filmstrips were running fast frame through her mind. She smiled her permission and acceptance and decided to flow with the experience.

Satron, the Keeper, said, "Joe-Joe is one of my multidimensional selves. Each self has an unknown number of probable lives and is free to manifest where it will. Joe-Joe's return to earth would be one of his probable stories in one of his probable lives."

Becka felt her head spin. "What are you saying?" she demanded, her courage increasing the longer she stayed in the presence of the angelic light-being.

"You are one of the multidimensional selves of your Light-Keeper," the Satron continued.

"In other words, you are but one manifestation of your Keeper. Each individual manifestation has many incarnations. Yet, all Keepers and their

Barbara Paul-Emile

manifestations are part of still greater entities. All are one. And so it is."

Chapter Eight

Encounters

$\mathcal{B}$ecka would not accept these confusing explanations, nor let the Satron off so easily.

"Tell me, Master," she responded, "what are multidimensional selves?"

Her tone was polite but there was a hint of skepticism.

In his gracious way, the light-entity showed appreciation for her interest and said, "You will see."

Coming quickly into focus out of a mist, she sees a scene of a black man working in a cane field. It is about noon and the sun is high in the sky. The day is hot and sweat runs from the worker's exposed back. He can not be more than twenty-five years old. His clothes, torn and patched, are little more than rags. He is without shoes and his body shows half-healed scars as from burnings and beatings. Becka watches him intently. He is focused and concentrated on his actions.

Barbara Paul-Emile

She sees his machete weaving its way expertly through the cane and hears the crackling sound of each stalk as it falls. She watches the rhythm of his movements as he cuts, strips and binds the cane. Even though there are more than a dozen people working near him, only his image comes clear.

Raising himself up to stretch his neck, the young man shades his eyes, looks up at the hot sun, and murmurs his displeasure in a language she does not know, yet completely understands. Out of the mist at the edge of the scene, comes a figure astride a horse. In his hand, he carries a long, black whip, which he waves freely from side to side as he rides erect, scanning the workers to his right and to his left. The man's haughty, cold face, though burnt by the sun, is still pale in comparison to the workers. He is European.

He is the "busha," the foreman. It is his job to see to it that the slaves work without respite. The seer tenses at his approach, for she feels the fear and hostility his presence brings to the scene. Without warning, she hears the thunderous crack of the whip as it lashes the African's back. She feels his body stiffen to receive the blow and sees the trickle of blood on the man's back as he bends again to the cane.

This scene did not need to be explained to Becka. It was slavery. The bullwhip, the symbol of authority and power, rested easily in the busha's hand. The location was immaterial. Yet, seeking confirmation outside of her own knowing, she asked, "Where is he?"

The Keeper answered quickly, "In the land you now call home."

"Jamaica?" The woman's voice broke and she trembled with anger as her disbelief melted into sorrow.

"Yes, Jamaica," the Keeper murmured.

Becka saw the scene melt at the edges and gradually fade away. A second image came swiftly to shape before she was emotionally ready to let go of the scene in the cane field. Images of large, stark buildings made of stone and bricks began to emerge.

The shaman finds herself in a cold land. This she can tell easily enough from the peoples' appearance and dress. They are sallow in complexion and are wrapped in heavy clothing, dark and somber.

One figure appears, clear and in full relief - a gentleman with European facial features dressed in a costume she has seen many times in old school books: dark colored pants that meet his white stockings at the knee, and a white high-necked shirt with ruffles covered by a black vest, buttoned down the front. Over these garments, he wears a black short coat that falls to his knees. His shoes, made of soft leather, are clasped in front by a bright shiny buckle.

"Who is this man? Where is this?" Becka shot out her questions, as she watched the figure move restlessly about in his small office cramped by stacks of dull-colored books and ledgers. The Keeper remained silent as though he was asking her to draw her own conclusions.

The middle-aged man, imaged before her, continues to pace back and forth nervously in his confined quarters. He soon strides out into a foyer with rounded archways built of fine stone. It is as though he anticipates meeting someone.

The figure is of medium height, stout with a robustness that indicates health. He appears to be waiting impatiently for someone or something. Becka feels the strain he is under, for he continues to pace back and forth and has taken to rubbing his hands together nervously while uttering curses under his breath. The shaman finds herself resisting becoming involved in the difficulties this man might be facing. Traces of the African's distress and anguish still linger in her aura. She refuses to allow herself to become interested in this man ... and yet, the level of tension and anxiety that emanated from him in his present circumstance is so high, that increasingly her own electromagnetic field is becoming unstable. She is beginning to pick up his transmissions and since he is less centered psychically than the African, she feels herself being drawn, irresistibly, into his emotional field. She feels his deep dread of some impending calamity.

In her struggle to stabilize her dream-body,

Becka realized that some regression had taken place. She was getting younger. She was now in the body of a fourteen-year-old girl. Noticing her astonishment at further age reduction, the Keeper smiled at her and changed form himself. Now he appeared before her as a European male figure, dressed in a loose monkish garment. Becka regarded him ruefully and thought, "I had better get used to this."

Her consciousness began to swim again. This time she felt a growing sensitivity to the area in the center of her forehead. Slowly, the images around her cleared and sharpened and her overall perception improved, as did her concentration. Miraculously, she succeeded in holding form. She felt more anchored and at ease. Becka saw the puckish smile on the countenance of the Keeper and intuited that he had again taken over the role of maintaining her dream-form.

The seer's attention turned once more to the scene before her.

An attendant, dressed similarly but less richly than the mature man, enters the room and says, " Sir, the carriage is waiting. Maybe there will be news." Without answering the servant, the nervous man spins out of the building, crosses the walkway and enters the carriage.

Becka noticed, with satisfaction, she was becoming better at maintaining a steady view of the scene. Any apprehension she had about understanding

Barbara Paul-Emile

languages was gone. Linguistic forms and structures all dissolved into inner "knowing." The content of the words streamed seamlessly into her cognitive faculties and she had immediate comprehension. She could enter and leave the consciousness of the figures before her at will. She could sense their feelings, see from their eyes, and hear with their ears.

The carriage takes off and the passenger is en route. The street, over which the wheels clatter, is covered by smooth stones, partly buried in the ground into which large ruts had been cut over time by the traffic. People dressed in heavy, drab garments crowd the walkways. As the carriage slows to a crawl, Becka sniffs the air and knows that she is near the sea. They must be approaching the docks, she thinks, as squawking gulls fly overhead. With accustomed precision, the carriage comes to a stop before a large and imposing building. The gentleman alights quickly and enters. He waves away a doorman who approaches him, and walks in confidently. He proceeds along a dingy corridor and, turning a sharp corner, goes down one flight of stairs to a larger but still over-crowded office.

"Any word yet?" he demands of the clerk who comes timidly to meet him. "Has the "Vaspère" docked?"

The answer is a subdued, "No sir."

"So," thinks the dreamwalker, "he is a businessman involved in sea trade." Inexplicably, she

knows that bad news awaits him.

This man has invested heavily in the contents of the ship and is worried about the survival of the cargo. The "Vaspère" has sailed from the West Indies and is on the last leg of its trip. There have been reports of storms at sea. The ship, long overdue, has yet to make port and deliver its merchandise. Becka is becoming good at picking up more and more of the character's thoughts and feelings. Right now, this merchant is consumed with anxiety and fear. His life-force seems to flicker on and off. All his vital signs signal stress.

He has been in business for many years and prides himself on being a sharp and wily trader. In the past, he has made much money, which brought him the trappings of success and respect from the business community. Now, he feels his financial future is in jeopardy. He has weathered bad storms before. But this time things are different. He is not sure that he can ride this one out.

Becka followed the merchant's thought-patterns as his awareness shifted to his family. A new scene, foggy at first, but increasingly better focused, came into view.

The seer sees an attractive home on a side street near a tree-lined canal. The door, similar to others on the street, is painted in a dark color and adorned by a large brass ornament in the shape of an anchor. Inside the house, the rooms are large and expensively furnished. There are a number of gilded paintings, marble sculptures and expensively upholstered furniture, all tastefully displayed. The laughter of children can be heard in an adjoining room. Before Becka can investigate, she finds herself in a beautifully wallpapered salon where a mature but still attractive woman, dressed simply in a white muslin gown, sits at a writing table. Becka moves closer to see what the woman is writing so intently. She is entering figures in a ledger.

For a moment, Becka merges her consciousness with the woman and senses the emotional turmoil within her. Murielle, as she is called, is not happy in her marriage. She feels that she has married beneath her social class and blames her family for arranging the alliance. She feels, further, that her husband cares more for business than for his family. As a result, they have few friends and no cultural or social life. The fact that her husband follows her household accounts so closely, despite all his wealth, does little to recommend him to her.

Again, Becka hears the laughter of the children, and follows the sound to a parlor where wooden toys, games, and children's clothing lay tossed about on the floor. Sitting in the midst of this disorder, are a boy about eight years old and a girl about six years, playing a game which involves tossing a small ball in the air and gathering up pieces of bones from the floor in time to catch the ball before it falls to the ground.

As a child, Becka had played a similar game in her time.

"I have won. I have won again," shouts the little boy happily, curls bouncing on the nape of his neck.

"You took my turn away from me," his sister responds with mock anger.

Becka watches as the children bickered, quarrel and start a new game. Safely anchored in their own world, they radiate joy and contentment untouched by the fortunes of their parents.

The seer wanted to stay longer in order to learn more about the household but that was not to be, for she recognized the warning sensations - the scene was beginning to fragment and she was drifting away.

The exploration into the lives of persons living in different lands, during different historical periods, was becoming of great interest to Becka. Traveling in her dream-body, she had been permitted, for reasons she did not understand, to share their thoughts and observe their physical and emotional struggles. She had been permitted to share their feelings and to experience life through their eyes. How much of this would she remember when she returned home to her own time? Becka did not know. She wanted to speak to the African to find out where he came from? Who were his people?

Recalling the last scene, she wondered about the fears of the anxious sea-merchant. She had vague intuitive feelings about his situation and wanted to know more about what actually happened. What was the outcome of his wait? What were his troubles? How did any of this connect with her search? She willed the docks and the wharf back into form but no new holographic images appeared. The scene along the canal continued to dissolve rapidly and the figures faded. Becka knew the signs. This representation was over.

Chapter Nine

The Dragon and the Hawk

*T*he dreamwalker found herself back in her favorite chair in the library. This time, the saintly dressed Satron was nowhere to be found. The room was enveloped by a strong energy vortex that magnified all emanations, and an electric-like substance bristled statically in the air. The display of books studded with gemstones and the art objects, ancient and precious, carried a garish yellow glaze that gave a caramel-colored gloss to the tapestries.

She felt claustrophobic, as the air became more oppressive. The seer had maintained her fourteen-year-old form, even though her understanding had been increased and the information in her memory banks had quadrupled. In actuality, the representation was accurate for she still felt a novice. She needed answers to questions. Answers that resolved to her satisfaction all that had taken place. She willed the presence of the Keeper. Nothing happened. "Well, am I on my own now?" Becka thought.

The silence in the room was deafening. Becka felt fearful, uncomfortable and, for the first time, terror formed itself like a coil around her dream-body. The power magnification of the room began to diminish and the lights to grow dim. Sounds, eerie and discordant such as she had never heard before, grew in intensity and became magnified. Just when she felt she would dissolve into the cacophony, again, there was silence.

The nightwalker listened intently and heard a soft hissing sound, such as one makes by forcing the breath through clenched teeth. The nightmarish monster that plagued the dreams of her youth had surfaced yet again. As a child, she had always dreaded those dreams and held a deep fear of being cornered, trapped and caught by something ... something grotesque. She heard the lumbering movement of a large mass and the rustling of scales. These were the very sounds she had heard on many a dark night alone in her bed. The heavy breathing, the sickening smell of malignancy and finally the piercing scream. Again, she was in the grip of this nameless fear. Becka felt herself losing form and the room began to close in around her.

The particles of light in her dream-body flickered tremulously. Whatever it was, it had finally found her and was outside the door. Did she have the courage to see its face? Did she have the power to confront and defeat it? The hissing grew louder. The beast's hot breath rose like steamy vapors from the open space at the bottom of the great door. The shaman heard the scraping of its claws on the floor.

Why not open the door and let it in? Face it and free herself of it once and for all, she thought. Becka felt the malevolent energy hovering, waiting. But what if she failed and was overpowered? The maelstrom of impacted negative energy in the room continued to build. A shiver rippled through Becka's dream-body as the light in the room dimmed further. She felt herself weakening.

Then Becka remembered that there were other means, other weapons. She was a shaman, a seer. The Satron, himself, had said so. She could use her inner force to rid herself of this predator. Firm in her belief in the powers she had been given, the shaman called for the Violet Flame of Transmutation and gave intention to activate the inflow of higher crystalline rays. Summoning her courage, the seer focused her consciousness, concentrated her powers and sent out a call for light:

Light Forms, Light Forms
Blazing, brilliant, bright
From your inner fires
Doth all the worlds arise.

The shadows show your absence
They call you back to being
Light Forms, Light Forms

Barbara Paul-Emile

Blazing, brilliant, bright
Where do shadows go when light appears?

With the sound of the incantation and praise-song still echoing in her mind, the seer slowly and with deliberation approached the great door, paused, and then swung it open. She faced a hideous swirling glare, so harsh, so terrifying in its intensity, that all was swallowed up in its distortion. Sickened, she felt herself forced back, and for a moment feared that she might be overwhelmed by the chaotic, destructive and unstable energy that sought to take control; but as the space around her filled with the harmonious resonance of iridescent rays from the higher spheres, immediately, the vortex of negative energy in the room began to weaken and to dissipate; the sickly yellowish glare, cast over the furnishings, began to disappear; and, once again, the room was bathed in sprays of crystal clear light.

Becka heard a distant wail and beheld the shadow-form of the unknown creature as it retracted its talons, threshed from side to side, and retreated from sight. Whatever this creature was, the shift in vibration had caused it to withdraw. It had given ground. A threshold had been crossed and she had gained access to higher levels of consciousness and resonation. The seer experienced a sense of release, reintegration and a powerful strengthening of her auric field. She knew how it felt to triumph.

As the scene crumbled, the shaman felt herself drawn away on fast moving currents of air. The presence of the Keeper was with her, even though she did not see him. She sensed it. She knew it. She believed it.

As questions took shape in the seer's mind, a response rose to her consciousness:

You are being shown what you must see
You are being given that which you need
Know that all is not as it appears
Take what you will, make covenant to share.

A translation or explication of the text flowed into her awareness: "You are being shown the complexity and the simplicity that is life. The time has come for you to know these things so you may impart to others. The time has come for you to become aware of the multi-layering of dimensions and the malleable nature of reality. All forms share a common source. All forms can be shapeshifted. You have asked your guides for knowledge and you have been answered." Becka pondered the message. She thought about the enormity of the implications and their relationship to her. ...

Thought-forms and images began to flow through her light-body. Rows of luminous geometric designs of various size, shape and pattern floated through her consciousness. Some of these designs, the shaman had seen before in her meditations and in her

Barbara Paul-Emile

dreams. There were zigzag lines, chevrons, circles, triangles and spots of light. She followed their movements without understanding their purpose.

In addition, the crystal and silver pellets, the specs of photon light, with which the Keeper had showered her at their first meeting, floated freely in the air. Each pellet seemed to possess an intelligence and was encoded in ways difficult to define. They formed themselves around her and clung to her auric body producing a feeling of confidence, exuberance and exhilaration.

Becka lost all sense of time and space. She felt her consciousness becoming soft and sponge-like. Her auric field grew large as her perception deepened. The spiritwalker felt herself supported and carried along with purpose.

Imperceptibly, landscape began to form itself about her and she finds herself floating over a great valley. The landscape is arid and there are few growing things, for the sun shines fiercely down on the brown, baked earth. The faces of the people are wizened and hard. Thousands have gathered at the base of a great tiered pyramid.

In silence, the people wait. Both men and women wear simple loincloths and loose-fitting garments. Most wear necklaces of stones and shells on their brown bodies, and coarse sandals on their feet. Their eyes are focused on the pyramid.

Becka knows whatever happened here would

affect them profoundly because they are as one in their intent. There is some apprehension but no fear. They believe with a firmness of faith and a will born of hardship that the cycle of pain will be broken. All eyes remain riveted on the pyramid.

Suddenly, out of an opening in the base of the structure, a woman steps forth: their High Priestess. Carrying an earthen jar in her arms, she begins her slow ascent to the platform atop the pyramid. On this dais, a flame burns and two priests wait.

The High Priestess, deliberate and graceful in her movements, keeps her eyes fixed on the summit. Oblivious to their presence, she passes the temple guards who lower their spears and kneel with great ceremony at her approach. Mid-way in her ascent, she is met by two priests clad in purple and white robes, wearing brightly colored beads about their necks and heavily plumed headdresses.

As the High Priestess attains the summit, she places the earthen jar on the altar and faces away from the people until the priests and guards descend to the base of the pyramid. Regal in her ceremonial dress, she wears a brightly colored, loose-fitting garment, which flows over her breasts but leaves her mid-torso bare. The skin at her waist, brown as the land she loves, is supple and taut. Her low-slung skirt is held by three golden clasps in the shape of a jaguar. On her chest, she wears the sacred emblem of the hawk; on her right shoulder is a red blanket that sways with the movement of her body. Tightly woven sandals cushion

Barbara Paul-Emile

her feet. Her tall headdress, made of colorful plumes and feathers, partially covers her thick black plaits.

The air of expectancy builds, yet the assembly remains silent. At the appropriate time, the High Priestess, sensing that the moment has come, raises her arms and turns to face the multitude. With one voice, the people cry out their salutation to her. She speaks the ritual blessing and the people chant their response in keeping with tradition.

High Priestess:	*May we be nourished by Spirit* *May we never be in want* *May there always be sufficient* *May we be loved and guided* *May we dwell in safety.* *May we give to the good of this land* *May we grow in light and truth* *May we be a part of earth's great web of peace.*
People:	*Hear us, Great Goddess, Hear us!* *We are your children* *You gave us life* *Nourish us* *Keep us safe.* *Hear us, Great Goddess, Hear us!*

Slowly the High Priestess turns her back to the assembly and faces the east. Holding the clay jar high, she pours the thick red liquid over the flames. The fire dies quickly and a thick column of smoke rises to the skies. The people cheer and burst into song:

Mother Goddess, Mother
Goddess
Loving Mother
Hold our land in your beloved arms
Cradle us, feed us
Make us strong.
Hear us, Mother Goddess, Hear us!

Let the rain clouds come
Let the thunders roar
Let the land be wet with dew
Let earth's moist body
Open to the seed.

Hear us, Mother Goddess, Hear us!

Glory to the Goddess, Glory!
Glory to the Goddess, Glory!
Glory to the Goddess, Glory!
Glory to the Goddess, Glory ...

Anticipation bristles through the crowd, for the people believe that the drought will break and the rains will come. They believe that their work in the

Barbara Paul-Emile

fields will be honored, now that the sacrifice of blood has been accepted by the Great Goddess. All has gone as it should, for the anointed one, the High Priestess, has done well. She has carried out the sacred rites at the traditional time and in the appointed way ...

Becka is mesmerized by the power and sanctity of the ritual. The chanting by the crowd is hypnotic. The High Priestess moves between worlds with dance-like movements, carrying out her duties with eyes open, yet in deep trance. She is able to place the sacred objects in their proper places on the altar and sing the ritual songs.

Abruptly, the High Shaman stops all activity and focuses her gaze. Becka, the dreamwalker, feels herself hit by a powerful blast of energy that surges like a wave through her dream-body and catapults her into physical reality.

The assembly gasps in astonishment and in awe at the two shining figures that now stand atop the pyramid. Where there was one before, now there are two. Becka finds herself dressed in a cloak of cascading streams of light and realizes that she has been drawn into a zone of magnified electromagnetic power. She feels the vortex of energy swirling, spinning, coursing up through her light-body. She shines with a radiance and a luminosity that equals that of the Priestess.

In her thoughts, Becka sends a prayer of thanks to the Keeper for his ministrations and turns to

Seer

85

gaze in admiration at her sister-seer.

Awe-struck, at first, the assembly at the base of the pyramid reads the signs and begins the ritual chant of the fertility rites:

Loving Mother Earth
Loving Mother
Hear us, Hear us!

We serve your Priestesses of Light
We honor your emissaries and guides

We draw to us your power
We draw to us your might
Hear us, Hear us!

The dreamwalker feels confident that she can control the power currents funneling through her. She steadies her consciousness and holds form.

The High Priestess shows no surprise at the entry of the visitor. Turning to address her guest, she utters the following words in greeting: "Welcome, Sister Spirit-woman. I bid you welcome to my sacred fire. You have come at my call. Welcome."

The dreamwalker returns the salutation and replies, "Woman, Shaman, High Priestess, I give honor to you and to your ceremonies."

The Priestess throws back her head and twice lets out the cry of the sacred hawk, her guardian bird. Her cries echo across the valley and into the mountains.

Suddenly two black hawks appear in the sky. They circle slowly returning her call and, as the crowd watches, one lands gently on the altar before the High Priestess. The other, its mate, continues to fly in large circles around the pyramid, high above the assembly. With the hawk nestled at her neck, the master-shaman turns back to the altar and with practiced motions builds the energy that sends multi-colored streams of light in arching waves out over the assembly.

Becka marvels at the magnificent display of the Priestess' shamanic powers and the ease with which she accesses alternate realities. The people gaze at the hawks, their sacred totem, and at the two shamans at the altar. Their hearts grow large with joy and pride, for they know that their High Priestess has summoned spirit-guests to their ceremony. The bird-god, Teitcan, has appeared to them before in just such a way. This presence is a good omen. They fall silent at the spectacle but are not afraid. They depend on their High Priestess to read all alien energy and to protect them if need be. Twice more, the Priestess sounds the cry of the sacred hawk and the sky grows thick with birds.

The altar and all upon it glow with a golden light. The air crackles with high-powered electrical charges. The Priestess honors the two great magnetic poles and, holding the staff painted with blue snake designs, taps four times on the platform, as though to awaken the earth. The electromagnetic field of the surroundings increases as the High Priestess, using her signature vibration, links together the energies of the inner earth.

Becka watches in silence as the master-shaman manipulates forces that could easily, if handled carelessly, unleash destruction and devastation. Portals were being opened and the ley or dragon lines of the land were being accessed. This interference would bring about great changes in atmospheric pressures. The correct harmonic balance must be achieved to bring about the desired results, for the subtle energies with which she dealt were powerful and volatile.

Sensing the tremendous acceleration in the electromagnetic fields and the growth in the strength of its currents, Becka understands that her role is to ground and to modulate the power that is being channeled to the Priestess from other spheres. She is the transformer, transducer, the lightning rod. Passing through her light-body, the energy is being stepped down. Becka knows her part. She has to focus her intention and hold form. Telepathically, she transmits her consent to assist Sister-Woman.

As spiraling currents and jolts of electricity explode into her dream-body, Becka sees the colors in her etheric field turn from indigo and gold, to brown and to red, and then are restored to their natural hues. In her consciousness, the seer feels the crystalline rock formations deep within the earth glisten and shake. She sees a ball of white light dance along earth's electromagnetic grid and trigger the atmospheric changes that are in the making. She feels the shift of the powerful earth energies and the trembling of the ley lines, and knows her work is done.

The dreamwalker feels her dream-body pulsing at a slower rate. Internally, she feels drained, spent, but she also feels exalted for she knows that the rains will come. The land will regenerate itself. Gaia's rhythms will be restored. As a gift from the High Priestess, Becka sees the people's future. She hears the sounds of splashing water, sees the green shoots raise their heads in the moist soil. She hears the people's songs of joy. All is well.

With the completion of the ceremony, the vortex of energy between the two seers begins to wane and to contract. Becka feels the settling of the currents, the emergence of new patterns and knows she is being released. Slowly her image begins to blur at the edges and to diminish. The High Priestess presses her hands together and gives the departing shaman the sign of love and unity. The assembly watches in silence, in awe, in respect, and in reverence.

Becka's consciousness remained long enough at the scene for her to see the Priestess make the final offerings and descend the steps of the pyramid. The High Priestess was met mid-point in her descent by her attendant guards, who stayed a step behind her until she reached the base where they escorted her into the inner temple.

Shortly, the High Priestess emerged to mount a painted platform, take her seat on a waiting chair, and be carried away by four bearers. The people cheered as she acknowledged them and followed behind her with songs and dances. The lead chanteur called out the lines and the people responded:

Chanteur: *We have ourselves seen the spirits at the altar.*

Response: *We have ourselves heard the scream of the guardian hawk.*

Chanteur: We have ourselves seen the Light-Being shining bright among us.

Response: *We have ourselves entered the great corridors of time.*

Chanteur: *Our land will be blessed and restored.*

Response: *Great is our High Priestess!*
                        Great is her lore!

Becka recalled how easily this sister-woman had manipulated realities. How graciously she had carried her great power. She remembered the feeling of comradeship they had shared and the energy produced by the alignment of their intent in their common quest. The shaman was reviewing her experiences when, unexpectedly, she felt the psychic tug that signaled the transfer of consciousness. She resisted the pull, for she wanted to spend more time in this place. On the far horizon, she saw dark clouds forming. The wind began to blow from the west and the temperature cooled. The shaman knew that the High Priestess had accomplished her sacred task.

Chapter Ten

Entering the Labyrinth

$\mathcal{F}$resh from her triumph, Becka was summoned back to meet the Satron. She couldn't help noting the growth of her awareness. As if in confirmation of her new status, her mind turned to Joe-Joe. What about Joe-Joe? Her mission had been to help the sick child lying helpless in his bed and to bring hope to grieving parents. Becka felt angry at herself for having forgotten her mission.

The Keeper watched the spiritwalker silently, following her thoughts as his power grid supported her shapeshifting.

Touched by her distress, he said, "Do not cause yourself pain, lady. You have not failed in your duties. You have been seeking Joe-Joe and you have met several of his multidimensional selves."

Becka's face fell vacant. She understood the import of the message well enough, but the meaning escaped her. For all her new learning, the Keeper's comments meant little to Becka. She heard the words but they conveyed no real information. The shaman had willed her return to her image of a mature woman. Now, with an adult's sensibilities, she felt slightly foolish that so much had escaped her. For, in spite of all that she had seen and heard, and in spite of the frequent comprehension augmentations she had experienced, she was painfully aware of how very little she actually understood.

Becka felt her head swim, as once again she began to process thought-streams emanating from the Keeper.

He said, "There is no cause for self-recrimination. You have done very well, but now, there are others you must see."

As the emission ceased, Becka's surroundings began to shimmer and the scene around her became scrambled. In that moment, she felt herself compressed and her consciousness drawn through a spiral into a small room.

Scanning the room, Becka absorbs the energy of the place. The dank air is saturated with a mix of emotions: anxiety, anger and grief. Before her, sits a young man on a small bench in a dirty cell, his head resting in his hands. The shaman approaches him but he does not sense her presence, for he is lost in a sea of pain and bitterness. This is a prison, the dreamwalker intuits. Even without the bars across the windows and doors, the feeling of despair and hopelessness that has built up over time is so strong that it infuses the very walls of the building.

On one wall of the cell, a hologram is beginning to take shape. Shadowy figures begin to appear. As the scene clears, there is sound and discernible motion. Becka sees the prisoner marching with others down a narrow cobblestone street. She cannot identify the country or the moment in history but the people in the crowd look as though they are wearing work clothes from the early part of the twentieth century. The young man, evidently one of the leaders, has a red banner in his hand. He, along with the marchers, sings songs, shouts slogans, and brandishes sticks and placards.

The crowd, filled with patriotic fervor and fiery bravado, is determined to hold a rally denouncing the authorities. Becka hears the word "dissident," understands its implication, and feels the danger around the gathering. As more information comes to her, she realizes that these are violent times and this young man stands against a repressive government. The dissidents know that the ruling elite has betrayed the people. Their birthright has been sold to foreign interests and the ruling class lives in luxury at their expense. Things have to be changed. In this peaceful and non-violent march, the intellectuals are demanding far-reaching economic and social change. Ultimately, they want freedom from oppression.

At the end of the street, Becka is shown what awaits the crowd. Trucks full of armed soldiers and

Barbara Paul-Emile

policemen form a barrier across the road. Some members of the military crouch beside their vehicles. Others place shields before their bodies. All are armed and ready. They know what they are expected to do. It doesn't matter that the "dissidents" are unarmed. It doesn't matter that what they have to do is tantamount to cold-blooded murder. Nothing matters. The orders have already been given.

Becka forgets for an instant that this is a re-creation. Energy begins to flow through her dream-body. She wants to stop the killing. She wants to alert, to warn the crowd of what is ahead. She wants to say, "No, no! Go back. Go back." But it is too late. The shooting has already begun. Many will be massacred, for the peace is now broken. The colors in the scene change, as the street runs red with blood and the screams of the wounded echo in the square. The ground is littered with the bodies of the dead and dying.

The young man, whose name she is given to know is Jan, is knocked to the ground in the struggle. As he lays there unconscious, she sees him carted up with several others and taken away in a van. After a mock trial, he, along with other leaders, is sentenced to be hanged. The scenes from the trial include the false testimony of paid informers who take care to embroider their lies with particularly vivid and graphic fabrications of the ways the military were provoked. They claim that Jan told them to kill and produce guns they claim were his.

As Becka looked away from the scene to study the man sitting before her, the images of his past began to blur and fade. The dreamwalker sensed the powerful mix of the prisoner's emotions: frustration at dying so young, anger and hatred for the corrupt authorities who lived by the laws of the stronger, and contempt for their hypocrisy, their lies, their endless greed. He had wanted to do so much and now it was all over. She felt his disappointment over his failure to accomplish his goals, and his grief for the loss of so many of his comrades in such a show of senseless brutality. "Was it worth the cost?" he was asking himself.

Becka wanted to comfort Jan. She wanted to say to him that others would come after who would pick up the fallen banner and take it to victory. She wanted to assure him that he was a brave man whose courage would not be forgotten. But all she could really do was mourn with him, for he was, indeed, young and his future would be taken away.

Suddenly, a ball of light enters the cell and Becka sees his body contract as a powerful energy blast rocks it. The surge is so strong that it brings him to his feet. Becka sees the spectacle and is amazed. The gray haze of despondency that had settled over the young man, begins to lift. The colors of his aura brighten, as the tension in his body is released. He straightens himself, walks about the room, and a calm settles over him. Becka merges her consciousness with his to follow his thoughts more closely.

It is evident that a transfer of power has taken place. An energy matrix has settled within his body that has raised his vibrational level. In future, he had only to access it, to lift himself out of depression. He is doing that now, for his eyes show him to be much more confident and assured. Jan's attitude toward his impending death is beginning to change. He begins to feel that his death and that of his comrades will not be in vain. They would die martyrs. Death would not be the end. Their sacrifice would be remembered and the revolution would succeed.

Becka wondered about the change in Jan and marveled at his transformation. Before she could speculate further, the prison scene began to wrinkle and to blur and the dreamwalker felt herself spiraling and falling. It was as though she was slipping back and forth in time. Different and varied scenes of persons unknown to her flashed across her mental screen. The images came so fast, she could not differentiate them completely. There was the figure of a beautiful black female entertainer singing before a large and enthusiastic audience; a boxer fighting desperately in the ring; and a traveler bidding good-bye to his family as he set out on a long journey. As the number of figures increased, the seer felt her vision dim and the scenes disappeared altogether.

Becka sent comforting thoughts back to the prisoner in his cell. A young man so vital, so alive - surely he could be allowed to live out his years. She could feel traces of his energy still with her. She wondered how he could be saved. A man of principle and high ideals, Jan would not accept freedom for himself if it was not offered to his comrades. Becka speculated on what the outcome to his predicament would be.

By some strange compulsion, the seer felt moved to seek help for this young man who was caught in a net from which there was no escape. As various impossible schemes to assist him floated through her thought-stream, Becka suddenly remembered who she was and what her mission was. She laughed ruefully to herself and thought that if she could not even find Joe-Joe, much less convince him to return fully to his body, how was she going to assist this man whom she did not know and who was under a death sentence. The recognition of her own impotence left her feeling frustrated and irritable.

The seer had been enthralled by the magical nature of the journey that had unfolded before her. She had been dazzled by the mind-exploding developments, the light shows, the time travels, the dramatic presentations. Now, she felt spent, exhausted and weakened by it all, full of questions for which she had no answers. She had seen great grandeur and beauty but she had also seen anguish and suffering.

What had happened to her mission? How could visiting all of these characters in their different lifetimes be connected to her search? Becka began to grow more and more uneasy and, as she became so, her form appeared more tenuous. It kept blinking on and off and she was finding it harder and harder to stabilize her dream-body. Finally, in distress, she focused on the library and on Satron. Within moments she felt the twisting, sucking motion that transported her between dimensions. She centered her awareness and was relieved to find herself seated once more before Satron, Light-Keeper.

Still dressed in modern clothes, the Keeper continued his conversation as though she had never left the room. Smiling at her amiably, he said, "In your search for Joe-Joe you have discovered his larger self and the figures that you have met are aspects of that larger self. All of these characters are intimately connected with Joe-Joe. Indeed, they are one with him. You will come to understand what these connections are. You have shown great courage on your part. Now you must learn patience. You have been preparing yourself for this journey for many of your years. You must follow the steps."

At the conclusion of the Satron's remarks, the image of the library began to dim and ultimately to melt like a popsicle on a hot day. Becka knew that she was off on another journey. She felt her own form contracting and her whole consciousness reduced in all its dimensions. Floating out of the room, the dreamwalker realized herself as a particle of light. Her dream-body dissolved, and she knew herself to be a shiny bubble of consciousness. She felt herself lifted along with Satron and released into the vastness of the cosmos.

The dreamwalker feels herself flying among the glittering stars, in stretches of somber darkness and in large expanses, where the mix of light and dark recede endlessly into the distance. She is a particle of light. A ray such as one would see refracted in a dewdrop on a leaf in the early morning. She is radiant and luminous. At ease with all things, she flows with creation. The sensation is at once exhilarating and exalted. There is no need for thought. No need for mental constructs. No need for meaning. No need for anything. One just was. One felt a part of everything. A dream within a dream.

Becka feels her progress slowing as she approaches a heavily clouded and massive orb. She flies with Satron through dense cloud cover and enters what she thinks is a planetary portal. She watches the Keeper identify the coordinates and locate the opening. Then she feels the pull of the magnetic field that draws them in. As both light-beings break cover, they find themselves floating over a thickly forested land.

From their high altitude, the contours and outlines of the surface offer surrealistic vistas and grand panoramic views. The dense cloud cover provides abundant moisture. Streams and waterfalls gush forth from vegetation-rich ridges and mountain- sides. The air is fresh and sweet. Satron and Becka circle and hover. Becka drops lower to take a closer look at the vegetation. The flowers are neon-lighted, with a startling incandescence. The trees are ringed in different colors and the soil is gray, flecked with red and yellow particles. So sharp and vivid is the contrast in shapes and forms, so compelling the incandescence, that temporarily Becka's vision blurs.

On the Keeper's signal, Becka wheels and flies off with him over one of the highest peaks that dominate the terrain. Soaring over the jagged, craggy vista, carried by moist air, the light-forms pulse and shimmer, appearing as glowing meteoric particles gently floating in the mist. They approach a valley, secluded and cloistered, where a light fog plays upon the mossy ground. Primeval and unsullied in its beauty, the colors here are softer and more muted.

Flowers and plants grow on this planet in colors, shape and form such as Becka has never seen. Soft and muted tangerines, magenta, subtle grays, violet-blues and silvery whites blend to create a startling pastel of hues. Plants cling close together and, from a single stem, grow flowers of different sizes, shapes and colors. The season has a pristine innocence about it. In her consciousness, the dreamwalker hears the Keeper say: "In Orion it is always Spring. Your earth was something like this once, before it lost its cloud cover."

Satron and Becka fly toward a construct made of a substance so transparent it hardly seems to exist at all. There are no doors, no steps, no stairs, no foundation or buttressing of any kind. It seems to float above the uneven ground, roofless, and open to the *sky. Bluish green light refracts from the corners of its transparent walls. Slowing to a crawl and hardly moving, the light-forms drift into the structure through the open roof. The Keeper manifests a table with flowers and fruits, accompanied by comfortable chairs. Becka studies the landscape and finds it so fantastical as to be beyond imagining. Deep musical harmonies can be heard in the distance and on the far horizon, twin suns burn dimly in the golden sky.*

The Satron and the shaman recreated their dream-bodies. Becka found herself in a simulation of the form she had on earth. She was wearing the same blue dress and turban she had worn to Mirri's house. The Keeper returned to his favorite form - that of the retiring philosopher. This time, he wore a plain brown robe. Satisfied with the accommodation and with the journey, the Keeper sat and looked quizzically at Becka. The dreamwalker looked away, not knowing what to say. So much had taken place. So much to know. So much to ask.

Tentatively, the shaman began posing questions to the Light-Being about this new place to which they had come. The Keeper explained that he found this domain restful and thought she might too. It was one of his favorite retreats and though he could have thought-traveled here in a moment, he preferred to journey in a semblance of time and space. The little expedition, he thought, would please her.

Chapter Eleven

Light Carriers

$\mathcal{B}$ecka was much affected by the Satron's willingness to share his private place of retreat with her. Looking about her in amazement, she wondered just how much of these mind-boggling events she would remember when she returned home. Would such wondrous episodes as her time and space-jumping become half-remembered dreams, where one recalled snatches and fragments without the ability to fit the entire sequence of events together? Her experiences were so vivid, so indelible, certainly, they could never be forgotten.

As the dreamwalker studied the surreal environment, she was impressed by the indescribable magnificence of the terrain. Through transparent walls, she saw the silhouettes of trees that took the shape of spirals as they grew. Twin and triple trees sprung from the same root, sharing a common support system. Each was the same, yet different. The rich variegated burst of colors - strong rust reds, cobalt, striped yellow-greens and purples - were a sight to behold.

"But what about Joe-Joe? What does any of this have to do with him?" Becka thought to herself.

The Light-Keeper responded, " You must ask him."

In the distance, the seer saw an approaching light-form. It shimmered in the light mist, barely skimming the air, and soundlessly floated into the room. Joe-Joe in his dream-body materialized before her. Becka's shock was almost equal to the joy she felt at seeing him.

Rising from her seat, "Joe-Joe," she said, "Where have you been? I have come to find you." She felt the exchange of energy between them as his consciousness merged with hers in welcome.

Becka continued, "Joe-Joe, your body lies on your bed barely holding on to life. If you remain here, it will die. You must return home with me and live out your life."

Joe-Joe's response flashed on her mental screen, "But I am alive," he said. "I am as alive here, as I am on earth. Yes, I am more so. Here I have great freedom and I am in touch with all my other multi-dimensional selves."

Becka studied the child. His dream-body was that of Joe-Joe, but his words were not those of a child. Puzzled, the dreamwalker looked closely at the boy and then at the Keeper. Was he speaking through Joe-Joe? she speculated.

The Keeper smiled quizzically and responded, "At this point in his life on earth, Joe-Joe knows that he must make an important decision. No one can make it for him. It was written by him before his birth that he would have this choice. He knew that one of his probabilities would be to return to us in this dimension or remain among you."

"Probabilities, choices," Becka said, her tone sharp with repressed anxiety, and her attitude combative, "What does it all mean? Why would he write this and when did this take place?"

She was becoming more and more irritated. Her patience was wearing thin. She wanted answers.

The Keeper continued, his manner unruffled by her outburst, "Joe-Joe has a number of probable lives he can lead. He could return to earth to live out one of his probable lives there, or he could remain here. Nothing is fixed. The past can be changed as can the present or the future. But that is another matter."

He returned to his subject, "Each choice one makes at any turning in life opens up different possibilities."

Satron paused as though gathering his thoughts. He went on to quote from one of his favorite poems, "*The Road not Taken*" by the poet, Robert Frost.

> *"Two roads diverged in a yellow wood,*
> *And sorry I could not travel both*
> *I looked down one as far as I could*
> *To where it bent in the undergrowth;*

Then took the other, just as fair
As having perhaps the better claim,
Because it was grassy and wanted wear;
Though as for that, the passing there
Had worn them really about the same. "

The Satron paused meditatively and continued, "The poet goes on to say:"

"Oh, I kept the first for another day!
Yet knowing how way leads on to way
I doubted if I should ever come back."

Becka had never heard of Frost, or of his poem, and was not interested. First, she was not sure she understood what the poem had to say and second, she did not see the relevance of this reference at this point. It was quite clear to her which road Joe-Joe should take.

The Keeper continued calmly, "Frost," he said, "was only partially correct. All roads *are* taken, for the possibilities of each moment must be explored and realized. The ones we recognize as 'real' are those that materialize in the third dimension. The other roads are taken by our probable selves. So narrowly focused is our sensibility, that we are not aware of the other choices that are developed and acted out in other dimensions."

At this point, Becka couldn't care less about all these dimensional explanations.

Barbara Paul-Emile

"What about Joe-Joe?" she wanted to know.

Turning to look at the child, she saw that he was dressed in short khaki pants and a plaid shirt such as he would wear on earth. His choice of clothing confirmed for her that he belonged in the village and in his parents' home.

The seer began transmitting furiously to the Keeper, but he was determined to complete his remarks. Smiling gently at both Becka and her charge, he said, "Only you, young man, can make this decision. What have you to say?"

Joe-Joe, who had been quietly watching the proceedings, appeared agitated and uncomfortable. It was as though he was not prepared for the level of complication the dreamwalker's presence had raised. He squirmed and twisted his fingers, "I have always had a difficult time making decisions. I chose the common illness of a flu followed by pneumonia so that I could have time to make up my mind about what I wanted to do." As though trying to create a logical argument, he said, "Now, let me look at some of my choices. First ..."

Becka was impressed by the child's expanded awareness. Then she remembered that in this dimension, Joe-Joe could still bear the image of a child and access the knowledge available to any light-form.

Joe-Joe continued, "If I remain here.... That is one probability. If I return to earth, that is another. Of course, myriad of probabilities spring from my return to earth."

Becka stopped him at that point and said forcefully, "Let us consider the likely probabilities, Joe-Joe."

He flashed her a grateful smile and said, "Yes, let's do that."

Satron appeared to be amused by the interplay between them. Both Becka and Joe-Joe ignored him and kept their focus on each other. Then unexpectedly, one of the transparent walls that surround them began to darken. Becka was, by now, quite accustomed to these exhibits and hoped that this one would offer material she could use to bolster her side of the argument.

The seer sees a bird's eye view of her village and her focus is guided to Sojey and Mirri's home. Evidently there is a gathering outside, for Duncan is leading a boisterous bout of hymn-singing and the cooking pots are on the fire. The men are huddled in groups, drinking white rum, while the women busy themselves preparing the food and speaking to each other in hushed voices.

Becka sees herself talking to Sojey who is leaning up against the gate. He thanks everyone, as he is supposed to do, for coming and for the gifts they brought. Although he appears to be in control of himself, he is barely sober, for he has been drinking heavily all evening.

The shaman hears herself say, softly, to the angry and grieving father, "Be thankful for the child's life. He stayed for nine years. It is right to mourn but remember you and Mirri are still a family."

But Sojey's face is hard and his voice bitter.

He turns his face away and says, "What did Joe-Joe do to deserve this death. He never hurt nobody in his life. Nobody. He was a good boy and he would have been a great man. I had such hopes for that boy. ..."

His voice drains off as he looks off into the shadows so that Becka might not see the tears. He continues, "Look at all the no-good people that live 'round here. Look at them and my boy is gone. I don't care 'bout nothing and don't bother to ask me to. And I ain't grateful to nobody for nothing."

Sojey had sought solace in rum and in his feelings of being abused by the fates. Even when his men friends approach and say companionably, "Come on man, have another drink. We poor people have only God to look to for support, you know. Come, man, sit with us and let us talk. The Lord giveth and the Lord taketh away. Joe-Joe is in heaven now at God's right hand. Him no feel no pain now," Sojey pulls away not wanting to mingle much with the mourners. He does not offer to help his wife either. In fact, he pays little attention to her.

Becka notices that Mirri's eyes were dry and red, having cried all of her tears by her child's bedside when she realizes he is gone. Now she carries her pain in her body. She thanks Becka for coming, for she feels the seer has done all she could. Mirri busies herself taking care of her son's body and making the funeral arrangements. Her women friends had come to her support. Silently, neighbors had arrived bringing roasted bread fruit, red bean and rice, saltfish and ackee, stewed goat, chicken and white rice, plaintains for frying, and bananas for cooking, herb teas and bottles of white rum. They brought extra cooking pots and pans, sheets and towels. They had brought hymn books and prayer books. But, most of all, they had brought stories of the pains they themselves had endured and the assurance that survival was possible.

As the figures disappeared and the scene vanished, Becka tried to gauge Joe-Joe's response, but he would not share it. He would not look at her and Satron seemed lost in thought. Before discussion could begin, other images came to life. Joe-Joe's house was again the setting.

Again, there is a crowd of mourners in the yard. There is singing and drinking. The women are preparing the meals and small groups of people exchange stories about the child who has passed. This time, however, there is a marked change. Sojey and Mirri are working together, helping each other.
Sojey moves among the mourners thanking and comforting them, but his eyes follow his wife as she hurries through the house. After the mourners have been fed, Sojey finds her alone in the kitchen and, seeking for a way to support her, pulls her close and

says, "It's just you and me, but we can make it. Joe-Joe would want us to." Bonded in grief, they cling to each other for a moment.

Events speed up and Becka sees the same house in later years. There is a child in the house, a girl, Vita, Mirri's niece, whom Mirri and Sojey have adopted and are raising as their own. The dreamwalker sees further into the future and is given to know that Vita marries and lives in the village with her husband and children. One of Vita's sons is named Joseph after Joe-Joe.

As the scene faded, the Satron said, "Death does not necessarily mean the end of joy or of life. We always face choices. Joe-Joe faces choices as does his parents. We grow from joy as much as from pain. Joe-Joe's family will survive if they choose to."

The seer listened to the Satron, but in this particular instance she was not completely convinced. She said thoughtfully, "Now what will actually happen if Joe-Joe returns. Let us see that."

She posed her question confidently because she foresaw the joy that would be in the home.

The images are quickly restored and Becka sees Joe-Joe at home with his parents and at play with his friends. She sees him as a young man preparing to go to Middlesex Training College to study business administration. The proud parents are helping him to pack up his belongings and are walking him to the bus.

Sojey, who lives for his son, is thrilled by the boy's achievements. However, he has accomplished little with his own life.

When next Joe-Joe comes into view, he is going to work at the local bauxite company where his days are full of petty administrative duties. After work, he plays soccer with the boys or goes to the local bar. Becka watches Joe-Joe grow older and for all the good times he is supposed to be having, he finds life to be empty. As the scene expands, Becka notices that time has passed for Joe-Joe and he is now about thirty-five years of age.

Family members feel that he has not fulfilled his potential. There is little focus to his life. Likable, easy-going but inwardly disappointed with himself, Joe-Joe is growing more internal. He meets a young woman, Gloria, a nurse, with whom he falls in love. Vivacious, lovely and ambitious for her own future Gloria is not certain that Joe-Joe is the man for her. Still she is drawn to him as he is to her; nevertheless, she is in no hurry to accept his proposal.

Abruptly, the presentation blinked off.

Again there was silence in the retreat as both the shaman and Joe-Joe shielded their private thoughts from each other about the scenes they had just witnessed. Becka withdrew quietly into herself. She realized that she had both mental and emotional sorting to do. Looking out through the transparent walls of the construct at the soft muted colors reflecting off the vegetation, she scanned the pea-green moss growing together with lemon-colored herbs and wondered what caused them to glisten with such iridescence. Their leaves seem to be coated by a thin sprinkling of gold and emerald dust. The air was perfumed with a light, fresh sweetness. Thoughts seemed to float through her consciousness, aimlessly.

The seer considered the pictures she has seen of Joe-Joe's life. They were troubling. Joe-Joe had not appeared particularly happy. In fact, his life appeared dull and rather uninteresting. Why would he want to go back with her? What would it take to draw him away from here? What would it take to bring him back home with her?

Nothing was quite as clear or as easy as she thought it would be. The complications were mounting and her mission was in serious jeopardy. Becka's energy level started to fall, and she found her dream-body blinking on and off as she contemplated the possibility of failure.

The spiral barks of the trees looked gnarled and stark. Each curve appeared in raised relief. Becka gazed at Joe-Joe reclining comfortably on a couch. He appeared serene and untroubled. The Satron sat with his eyes closed, listening to the music that drifted in from the stratosphere. Becka sent him a message asking him for assistance.

Rousing himself, and focusing his gray unblinking eyes on her, he said with calm assurance, "Joe-Joe will make his decision, do not fear. But there is much to be considered. We must have a consultation. This must be discussed further."

Becka thought that they were already having a consultation, which was not, from the look of things, going in her favor.

Once again the shaman experienced the signs of an impending psychic journey. Her vision began to blur and her consciousness shift, as a scene took shape before her inner vision. This time, the external walls did not darken. No projected screen was present. The seer closed her eyes and saw the house by the canal and, instantly, she was there.

The street is the same one she visited before. The scenery has not changed. The house, however, appears smaller, less opulent. There are fewer pictures on the wall and fewer rugs on the floor. Clearly, financial retrenchment has taken place. Becka sees the children asleep comfortably in their cozy beds. Their father, the merchant, lays resting peacefully next to his wife, Murielle. Becka watches them quietly, not really knowing why she is here.

Then, as though conscious of her presence, the merchant's dream-body, diaphanous and transparent in substance, slips out of his body and rises to a seated position on the bed. Separating itself from the physical body, it stands upright in the room. In appearance, it is identical to its physical counterpart that remains asleep. In action, it is lighter, freer and more maneuverable, being able to pass easily through

Barbara Paul-Emile

substances considered solid in the third dimension. The light-being doesn't appear surprised to find Becka there.

Abruptly, the shaman feels a psychic tug and senses that she is being summoned back by Satron. She turns to go, only to be followed by the dreaming merchant. Glancing back at the bed, Becka notices that his spirit-guides, with wings folded, are in attendance by his bed and will await the return of his dream-body. Murielle, exhausted by the demands of the day, sleeps heavily and dreamlessly, moving ever so slightly to shift the weight of her body closer to that of her husband. The room is enveloped by a mixture of light and shadow, as moon beams, streaming through the slats of louvered windows, make silver gray patterns on the wooden floor. Feeling again the tug at her consciousness, Becka leaves the house, followed by the merchant's dream-body, floating effortlessly through walls and doors, invisible to those in physical form.

The dreamwalker, responding to the Keeper's call, found herself, along with her companion, back in the cloister-like transparent structure on the planet Orion.

Chapter Twelve

The Gathering

*W*hile Becka was away, other light-beings had arrived. The visitors turned to greet her and the merchant as they materialized in the room. The dream-walker looked at the gathering and recognized several of the visitors. Standing not too far from her was the young African she had seen in her first vision. He smiled at her and immediately she felt a kinship with him. With great courtesy, he transmitted his name as Mosca. Tall and imposing in his appearance, he stood out among the guests. He wore work-clothes suitable for the hot tropics: loose pants and shirt, simply cut, and made of coarse blue material. In his hand was his machete, sharpened to a glistening point.

To his right, stood the High Priestess dressed in a diaphanous cloak of a rich burgundy. She appeared to be lost in her own thoughts and looked off into the distance through the clear walls. She was without her ceremonial headdress; however, she wore the same large broach in the shape of a hawk that Becka had seen at the sacred site. Her flowing skirt was low slung over her hips and the smocking in her loose-fitting bodice was edged in gold. Striking in her beauty and appearance, she seemed unaware that everyone was stealing glances at her. Her magnetism lay not only in her beauty but in the air of mystery that surrounded her.

Jan, the young man of whom she had become so fond, stood in the far corner of the room. He appeared pale and his auric colors were muted. His face was expressionless; his attitude one of stoic control. He was experiencing a difficulty well known to Becka: unstable energy fluctuation. His dream-body tended to blink on and off unexpectedly. He stood a little distance away and was detached from the group. No one approached him. Closer to her was Joe-Joe, still manifesting his boyish dream-body, deep in conversation with the Satron.

Well, thought the dreamwalker, this is an interesting group. A stillness settled over the room.

The Keeper ended his conversation with Joe-Joe and, turning to the group, said, "I welcome you here and I thank you for coming. I called this meeting to discuss Joe-Joe's dilemma. As you know, he must decide whether he will return to earth or remain in this dimension. I feel that nowhere would he find better advisers than you. Becka, seer and dreamwalker, has come to find him and to encourage him to return to his family, to whom he is most dear."

Surprisingly, it was the merchant who spoke first. He gave his name as Stefan. Addressing himself to the gathering as a whole, rather than to Joe-Joe specifically, he said; "Why should the boy go back only for his family's sake. One must live for oneself. To live life well, one must have something that is important to one's self. In my case, I have my business. It is my life. I am considered to be a successful man. I have no wish to leave life now. Of course, there are hardships but they can be mastered. Success never comes easily. What does this boy wish to do with his life? That is the question."

All eyes turned to Joe-Joe who looked at the Satron and squirmed uncomfortably but said nothing.

The High Priestess broke away from her rêverie and looked directly at Joe-Joe. "Child," she said, "which probable life do you wish to live? Upon that choice does all else depend."

Becka monitored group interaction intently. She remembered how dull Joe-Joe's life appeared. What would he choose to do? Here was that phrase "probable life" again. What did the Priestess mean by it? Satron had already shown what would happen in Joe-Joe's life if he lived. Nothing could be done about that now. Regardless of what Stefan said, the child had to come back home because he loved his parents and they loved him. That was all there was to it, Becka thought to herself.

The Keeper appeared pleased with the High Priestess' remarks and, smiling at her, said; "You are correct, Zalca. Within a broad spectrum, everyone creates his own reality. So it is with all humans. Each person chooses the drama he or she wishes to experience. The probabilities of a given lifetime are many. In the context of family situation, country and culture, each entity has many choices. Joe-Joe has chosen to incarnate on an island in the Caribbean, rich in history and its mix of cultures. Its people have come from all parts of earth. Certainly, there is much one can chose to do there."

Becka gave tacit support to the opinion transmitted by Satron and for a moment her thoughts turned to her island home. Slowly, the atmosphere, scents and images of the Caribbean began to drift into her consciousness and a dreamscape began to coalesce around her.

Becka hears the call of the seabirds, the gushing sounds of rivers tumbling through rocky gorges, and the splash of the waves lapping the sandy white beaches. In her mind, she sees the waving cane fields, the spreading breadfruit trees and the flaming Poinciana with its cluster of bright red flowers. She smells the astringent, spicy pimento trees whose berries are left to dry in the hot sun. She tastes the sweet-tasting, orange-colored papaya and the yellow melon, whose fruits grow in clusters on a branchless trunk.

Becka smells the sweet pungency of fever grass teas and hears the laughter and shouts of women

standing mid-stream on wash day with their dresses
rolled up to their thighs, their dark legs glistening wet
with rivulets of spring water.

The seer sighed. She felt the longing for home
as a pain and knew that she could not bear to be away
much longer. She looked closely at Joe-Joe and
wondered if it was so with him. Did he also feel the
pull toward home? Did he remember? Did he
remember? Although he looked alert and focused, his
feelings were masked, his eyes were guarded and he
said nothing.

Jan, standing apart, was also quiet. He had
contributed little to the conversation so far. Yet, it was
clear that nothing escaped him. Moving from his
position in the far corner of the room, he came to the
center. Facing everyone, his face intense, his voice
firm, he said, "Life is worth living when one believes
in something. Not just anything, but something of
value. Not useless success or shallow acclaim, but
something that makes life better for all."

He threw a scornful glance in the vicinity of
Stefan. "The mere accumulation of wealth is not a
worthwhile reason for living," he continued.

"This obsession leads to greed which ultimately
demeans the spirit and makes barren the soul. Life
demands more of us than this."

The merchant showed his disagreement by
turning his broad back to Jan, who ignored him and
continued: *"To truly live, one must have a cause*

Barbara Paul-Emile

greater than oneself. Larger than one's own life. Such a cause must be large enough to embody the good of fellow human beings. This does not mean that we need all be called 'great,' but we must do what we can where we can."

Hearing the tone and tenor of Jan's remarks, the merchant could restrain himself no longer. Turning to look at the group and then specifically at Jan, he said, "What will those sentiments get anyone, I ask you? What you say is youthful foolishness, sir. Pep-rally talk, nothing more. That is not the way the world works. That is not the way at all. I am my own cause. Who thinks about me, if I do not? Who? You tell me that. No one. No one at all. People look up to the successful ones, regardless of who they are. They are obsequious to you in the hope that you will help them succeed as well. Or, better yet, give them what you have. Don't tell me about the world, sir. *I know it.* I have had wealth and I have lost it as well. The only reality I want to create is one in which I am successful, wealthy and admired. That is happiness. There is nothing else."

Jan thought about Stefan's response and then said, patiently, "There is *everything* else. You know nothing about this because of the choices you made in your life. Have your ever known happiness?"

"As much as anyone else," Stefan responded. "When my business goes well, I am happy and content. When I am able to handle my obligations, I am happy. Is there more?"

"There is much more," Jan replied. "Happiness has nothing to do with what one has or does not have. It is a feeling in the soul. It is the joy of life welling up from within one. How much one possesses has nothing to do with happiness. Your focus on the material has reduced the quality of your life and hampers any enjoyment you can feel."

Joe-Joe watched and listened carefully, his eyes darting from one speaker to the next.

There was a nobility about Jan that drew respect from his listeners. Becka felt proud of him, for she agreed with his point of view.

Feeling the audience shift away from him, Stefan said loudly, with studied contempt and with an acute sense of irony, "What happiness have you ever known? You have lived your life for ideas. What have they brought you? You are now facing your death."

The pain of his remarks registered on Jan's face. Becka flinched. "How could Stefan know Jan's fate?" she asked herself.

The High Priestess approached Stefan and, looking directly at him, said, gently, "You fear death. This much is clear and you feel that others should as well. But there is no death. *Death is an illusion.* How can spirit die? And you are spirit. In death you merely leave your mortal body behind as you do now in your dream-time. The mortal body is the great earth goddess' gift to you. You return that body to Gaia to replenish her and then you come home to spirit. Jan need not fear the transition."

Barbara Paul-Emile

Becka was impressed by the matter-of-factness with which the Priestess spoke. She, herself, believed in the after-life but never had she heard anyone speak with such confidence and authority on this subject. Stefan looked at the High Priestess, then glanced away and scowled. "She is right," thought Becka, "he is afraid."

The Priestess continued, "Death is a transition, a gateway. Nothing more. After a life on earth one merely returns to spirit."

Stefan looked at Jan and said, "I do not hear Jan saying that. He is to die soon, maybe tomorrow. I think that he is afraid. What did he get out of life? All that talk about freedom for people. What will they do for him? The poor creatures who cannot feed themselves should concentrate on bettering their own condition, not on freedom and other such complex and complicated philosophical concepts. Jan and others like him have misled them. I give them work. Jan gives them platitudes and useless, dangerous ideas. What does he get for all his efforts? Death!" Stefan laughed harshly with cynical detachment.

The High Priestess continued to regard Stefan calmly. Her gaze was steady, yet non-judgmental. The man braced himself and remained in her presence as though magnetized. She said softly, "Death is a natural part of life and after a life well lived, it is an honor. Jan has carried out his contract and has lived well."

Encouraged by her remarks, Jan rejoined the discussion. "There were times I felt that my stay on earth was incomplete and I grieved over my departure," he said. "Yet I know that this is how it should be and my feelings of anxiety have left me. On particular occasions, during my first days in prison, I felt that I would go mad. Anguish and frustration over the loss of my comrades plagued me. I felt alone and abandoned. During those dark times, strength always came to me and my balance was restored. I give thanks now for the courage that came to me."

The Priestess listened quietly to Jan. Then she went over and touched his face. She looked into his eyes, smiled, and said, "Those were the times, I came to you and gave you strength, little one. I felt your grief. I gave you love. I anchored and centered you. There is nothing to fear. I will be with you on that day. Sense and see me, for I will be there with you."

Becka noticed that the Priestess' proximity had caused Jan's aura to brighten and to become enlarged. His store of light energy had increased. She called to mind her visit to his cell. She remembered his fatigue and his despondency and the emotional transformation wrought by the sudden power charge that surged through him. She wondered if that gift had been given by the High Priestess?

Jan's auric field pulsed rapidly and a shower of tiny photon pellets materialized around him, dissolving into his light-body. He held out his hand to Priestess Zalca. She took it and whispered something to him that no one else heard.

Stefan regarded the exchange between the two

with great suspicion, his eyes hooded. As the Priestess moved away from Jan, she turned to the merchant and said, thoughtfully, "Now how do *you* feel about death, dear one?"

Stefan looked at her and then glanced away uneasily. The High Priestess kept her gaze on him and asked pointedly, "Are you able to feel for others?" Then very gently, she said to him, "Tell the others what your trade is."

Stefan recoiled from her. Immediately he became the center of interest. Everyone in the group wondered what the Priestess intended by her question. Jan, who was standing next to Mosca, walked over to the Satron and sat next to him. Stefan looked out through the transparent walls and gave no answer to the questions put to him. There was silence in the room. Every one waited. Instinctively, the merchant looked to the Satron for help. Their gaze locked.

The merchant got up from his seat and, speaking to no one in particular, said in a low voice, "I am a trader. My business is legitimate and honest. I must make a living, and I do."

"Now, tell them what it is that you do," Priestess Zalca insisted quietly.

The discomfort of the man grew. Fear and foreboding settled over the room like a pall. All eyes were riveted on Stefan who pressed his palms together as though in prayer and placed them over his pursed, protruding lips. How, thought Becka, could a man who spoke so glibly and confidently be so determined to remain silent? What did he do? How did he make his living?

Again the Satron looked at him and this time the merchant dropped his hands to his side and spoke, albeit reluctantly, "I invest in cargo. Workers are needed in certain parts of the world and I invest in cargo." There was silence while his remarks sunk in.

Jan was the first to speak, "Are you saying that you trade in *human cargo*? You are a slave dealer? Are you one of those who profit from the suffering and death of others?"

Stefan made no response.

Mosca who had been seated, rose to his feet. He seemed stunned, dazed, dumbfounded. Prior to this revelation, Becka noticed that he had followed the proceedings with a half-smile on his lips, only partially committed to what was taking place.

Now, with two steps, he was in Stefan's face. The merchant seemed to cringe and backed away at his approach.

"Are you a dealer in slaves? Tell me. You dog! You excrement! Are you one of those who profit from my people's pain?" His voice was hoarse. His face contorted with anger. Even though Stefan was in his dream-body, he looked at Mosca's machete and shrank back.

"Do you know what it means to be a slave? What part do you play? Where does your profit come in? Do you pay those who waylay us and trap us and sell us to the ship's captains? Or do you profit along

Barbara Paul-Emile

with the plantation owners from whatever our labor creates? Where do you come in?"

Since Stefan would not answer, Jan offered an ironic response. "He comes in wherever he can. What does he care, so long as he makes a profit?" Jan's sarcasm seemed to be more insulting to Stefan than Mosca's rage and the merchant seemed ready to respond to the revolutionary. He tried to walk over to where Jan was, but again Mosca was in his face.

The African said calmly, "Do not walk away."

Seeing that there was going to be no escape for him, Stefan said, pleadingly, "My business is legitimate. It is legitimate," he insisted stoutly. "I invest in ships and in sugar. That is all."

"But what is carried in the ships and who makes the sugar?" Jan inquired, "Do you care? No wonder you fear death. But you need not, for you are already dead in spirit."

The High Priestess looked at Stefan and said, "No, he is not dead in spirit. He has yet to access his spirit. He fears to reach beyond the material world he loves so much. This is not the first time he has visited me in dreams and we have talked about this. The issue he faces has to do with personal power and self-worth. His view of himself is inextricably bound up with the opinions of others. He feels his business is legitimate because the social consciousness of his time accepts it."

"And well it should," Stefan answered. He was feeling more and more belligerent now that he was a safe distance from Mosca, and memories of his financial successes came back to him. He remembered the time *cargo* had to be jettisoned over the Atlantic because of illness aboard. He remembered his struggles with the insurance company that had insured the cargo. The underwriters had at first refused to pay and many of his associates had accepted the situation, but not him. He did not. In the end, he had won out and made money on the venture. That money bought him the new house and its furnishings. He was admired and respected for his resourcefulness. This group knew nothing about business - nothing at all.

Jan watched Stefan with disgust. The slave dealer's thoughts were now open enough to be read. It was clear that the man felt no shame. He took pride in his dealings. "How can beings such as these live?" Jan asked himself.

"By not feeling," the Priestess answered, ruefully. "By not feeling for others. Not all humans are capable of '*feeling.*' Those who commit the most heinous crimes are not capable of joining with the consciousness of others and feeling their pain. The ability to feel connected or to understand connectedness with others is a matter of psychic and soul development."

The High Priestess and Jan continued to speak but Mosca did not hear them. His face became a mask. He looked at Stefan and anger coursed through him like the hard white rum he drank at night with his compatriots to stop his mind from thinking. He

Barbara Paul-Emile

looked about him, not knowing where he was. This was indeed a strange place, for no one here had physical bodies including himself. Nevertheless, he wondered how he could go about ridding the earth of this vermin that crawled on it in the shape of a man. Never had he been so close to one of those who had made his life such a misery. Never had he heard such a brazen attempt to justify the suffering he had endured. Where he lived, the owners and their foremen went armed for they knew of the hatred that met them at every turn.

Once, he was told that to be a trusted worker in the master's house one had to be born into slavery, with no memory of freedom. Maybe that was true. But even there, the masters were not safe because he had heard that these trusted ones sometimes learned the way of the masters and used it against them. What was he to say? What was he to do that would ease his pain? His memories of his family, of Sika, his wife, cut through him like a knife. She was never out of his mind. Was she dead? Had she survived the crossing in the stinking death ships? At night, he would hear her breathing and feel what they had shared together. These people had taken everything away from him, and then to talk about *profits*!

Mosca guarded the expression of his feelings, but all in the room watched him, eager to share his thoughts. He was sure the Priestess and the old man could, but he did not know about the others. Without intending to, Mosca found himself speaking. The words came hard to him and he spat them out as he did the brackish water he used to rinse his mouth each morning.

"You, Stefan," he said "stand before me and say that you are one of those who live and make profit off my labor. You tell me that without remorse or shame? Listen now to me. I was taken by night from my village on a day when some of my brothers were away at the hunt and the vigilance required for our day to day survival had exhausted us. That night is branded on my mind forever, as my skin was later branded by the hot iron of slavery. That night I had told my mother, Afoa, to sleep in my dwelling with Sika for protection. I had stayed awake on guard most of the night. But by morning, I was tired and went outside for water to wash my face and keep myself awake. Before the water touched my face, I felt the gun at my back. I was taken and so were my wife and mother. The others in the village were taken as well and our dwellings burned to the ground.

"Chained to each other, I, and most of the people I had ever known, were dragged on a four-day march to the coast. My mother died on that march and was left behind, unburied. Before boarding the ships, we waited in the stinking holding cells divided by gender. I could not see my wife. I know not whether she was shackled and taken aboard the same ship as I, for one, never saw her again."

Mosca's body sagged and his eyes burned with unshed tears. No one spoke. All waited for him

Barbara Paul-Emile

to continue.

"On board that floating hell they called a ship, I saw men and women, packed like stinking fish in a wretched basket, die daily. Our village chief sat and refused food. With pliers and tongs the sailors tried to force the filthy food down his throat. But he steadfastly refused. He was whipped and he was tortured but he refused. On the fourteenth day, he died by the strength of his will. I wished then that I had learned the ways of the shaman, so that I could have died also. But that gift was not bestowed on me. I was cursed with life. When our ship docked in the waters of the Caribbean, so strong was the stench of excrement and refuse, so odious the smell of the sick and dying, that our ship was not allowed to dock in the harbor until a cleaning, such as it was, had taken place.

"At the point of sale, our bruises were covered with the polish that cleaned boots and we were whipped and told to dance. We were examined like cattle for our strength and weaknesses. I was designated able-bodied and fetched a handsome price. I can still see the smile on the face of the auctioneer as he shouted out my sale price. I knew my life was over. I knew I would never see my land or my people again. I thought of my mother, dead, and denied the rites of burial.

"Who are these people? I ask myself. Why are they so cruel? In what do they believe? I am made to work from two hours before sunrise to two hours after sunset. I am considered inhuman: a beast of burden and an inferior creature. Who are the inferior creatures - my captors or myself? I listen to this man speak of his profits and his love for himself. What sort of creature is this? I came over on the slave ship, *Manmouth*, which, I understand, serviced the entire Caribbean, stopping at various points along its route to drop off 'cargo.' I have lost all that matters to me. *All*." At this point, Mosca stopped. He made an attempt to continue but could not.

Jan moved to stand beside Mosca as though to embrace him. Like most of us, he did not know what to say or do. Joe-Joe left the Satron's side for the first time and joined both men in a show of support. Becka saw a shower of crystal pellets, such as she had experienced many times, fall on Mosca's dream-body which appeared badly rent and torn. Her heart went out to him. This is pain, thought the shaman. Oh God, this is pain. Stefan pretended to ignore the proceedings and looked out the window as though he wished he were anywhere else but there.

Again, it was the Priestess who acted. She took the golden hawk pin from her bodice and placed it on Mosca's chest. She embraced him and said, "You must have courage and live this life, Mosca, for this is the life you have chosen. You have the strength to go through this experience of loss, abandonment, and abuse. We are ever with you. As for Stefan, release the anger you bear him. There is good within him but he is afraid to honor it. He can change his life-path if he but chooses. On the other hand, he is learning much from this life and so are we. His next, probable life, which is on-going now, of course, is quite different."

Chapter Thirteen

Time Trials

$\mathcal{B}$ecka felt her mind beginning to reel and she was definitely showing signs of sensory overload. Mosca's recounting of his experiences had moved her deeply. It was as though she had lived those years with him. The spiritwalker found herself speaking: "Nothing," she said. "No amount of gain is worth the destruction of other human beings. I thought I knew about slavery, but I know now that I know nothing at all. I will never forget what Mosca has said here this day. I will carry his words within me."

Turning to the Satron, the seer said, as though looking for a way to accept the past, "What choice do we have about which life we live. This is the life we have. What other probable life is there? I know that we do not die. I know that we only leave our bodies behind. But probable lives? What does this mean? Probable lives have been referred to more than once here. What is the meaning of this phenomena?"

Barbara Paul-Emile

Again there was silence. All looked toward the Satron, who sat quietly listening to the discussion. He motioned the seer to come and sit by him and speaking to her in calm but compelling tones, said, "Becka, this meeting is in Joe-Joe's interest, but it is in your interest as well. Listen carefully. There are no endings and no beginnings. All has been and will always be. *All time is one.*

"Past, present and future do not exist outside of the time/space continuum of your dimension. Time is experienced as linear only in the third dimension. As long as you are in this sphere, you will experience time as such. Think now and remember that even in the third dimension, your feelings and emotions affect how you experience the passage of time. Sometimes you experience time as slow and other times you feel that it is speeded up. This recognition should tell you that time is mutable and not fixed." He waited for what he said to sink in.

The Keeper continued, "There is only the eternal *now*. Whatever you do in the eternal *now* can affect what you consider to be past, present and future. *Now* is the only time there is. Outside of this dimension, all is taking place at once. In your dimension you can, through memory, perceive all of the stages of your life at once. You can see yourself in your childhood, youth, maturity, and in your old age. You can manipulate time and memory in this way. In your imagination, you create alternate versions of all these stages of your life and see them as real.

"In other realities, all of these seemingly linear events are, in fact, taking place at once and all of those imaginary versions that you create are probabilities that are manifested in other dimensions. Hence, all probabilities are followed up and acted out. These dramas do not, of course, manifest in your dimension. This would be too confusing for you. It is enough to ask you to keep your focus narrowly tuned to your own life in your time.

"In this context, then, understand that all the beings in this room are living in different epochs and yet these epochs are taking place at the same time. Further, there are probable versions of themselves existing in other worlds. There can be contact between different entities living in different time frames because thought does not occupy space or time."

Becka paused and then repeated, thoughtfully, "The same time? How is that possible?" Then she answered her own question before the Satron could respond, "That is not possible."

She looked at the others as though for confirmation. No one spoke.

The Satron smiled and continued, "Each being here is alive at this moment, for each moment intersects all time-lines. Outside of this dimension, time is experienced as one. Only on earth is time experienced sequentially. The High Priestess, Zalca, is living more than five thousand years before your time, when goddess energy permeated the earth. During that time, people understood their relationship with nature and with the Mother Goddess. This was the time before the spirit of the masculine became the dominant force and shaped the world you know. In earlier times, women were the keepers of the flame. I offer no judgment here, because both streams of energy are of value when held in balance."

Then, glancing at the High Priestess, he continued, "When you visited her, you thought that it was an exercise in shapeshifting. It was, but it was also more than that. Zalca is as alive as you are now, and her lifetime parallels yours. This is true for all the others. Stefan and Mosca live in the eighteenth century. Jan is in the twentieth. You and Joe-Joe are in the early twenty-first."

Satisfied that she had heard him, the Keeper continued, "All of these beings are in touch with each other."

Becka struggled to comprehend what the Keeper meant. Her consciousness felt as though it would implode. "How can this be true?" she thought. "How can this be true? What about the past, present and future?" The seer was finding it difficult to discard knowledge she had considered hard fact. Her dream-body began to dim and her energy to fluctuate.

Fundamental constructs upon which her world rested were falling apart. Becka could accept her present experiences in the context of the malleability of dream-travel, but not when these new principles began to reconfigure her day-to-day reality. She had made demarcations between the physical world and dream-time. She knew where one ended and the other began. Was she to believe that time, as she understood it, does not exist and that there is only an endless *now* - no past, no future, no time sequences?

The High Priestess watched the internal struggle in which the seer was engaged and honored her for the courage it took to contemplate this paradigm shift.

Approaching Becka, she said, "There is no past, no present, or future, dear one. *All time is one.* In the third dimension we experience the passage of time as a progression. Of course, one's focus must be precise to maintain this narrow band of frequency. Most humans, however, accomplish this quite comfortably. Those who do not, are often considered insane in your society and are locked away and are treated with drugs. Some of them are not mad, truly. They have merely moved out of their narrow band of frequency."

She laughed softly and continued, "Many have simply begun to access alternate realities and dimensions."

At this point, Becka thought that she had lost her range of frequency completely. She fell silent, not knowing what questions to ask or how to interpret the answers.

Stefan, who had been sitting off by himself feeling ostracized and left out of the discussion, rejoined the group and said with a smirk, "So much nonsense, gibberish I have never heard. Time as one.

Barbara Paul-Emile

All nonsense. Everybody knows that today is today and tomorrow is tomorrow. How can all time be one? How would we live? Tell me that. I know myself to be living day-by-day and that is all."

Becka sensed that the merchant was displeased with the Satron for not helping him with the High Priestess' queries. He had considered his profession to be his own private business. At this point, there wasn't much that he would agree on with the Satron or anyone else for that matter. Becka detected his flamboyant defiance as an attempt at self-protection. He feared both the High Priestess and the Satron. He felt that they knew more about him than they should. Further, he viewed Mosca as a threat and responded to his powerful indictment by hiding behind the mask of a brave face and a cynical demeanor.

Becka had watched him closely while Mosca spoke and had seen the signs of anxiety and shame that Stefan sought to conceal. He feared Mosca. Jan, on the other hand, the merchant despised and dismissed as an idler, a talker, a dangerous busybody who got himself and others into trouble. He felt that Jan had probably never done a creditable day's work in his life. He disliked intellectuals in general who, having no hold on reality, were always spouting new ideas and wanting to change things.

"You, Stefan," the Light-Keeper said, "are not yet aware of the multi-layered world in which you live. In what would be considered your previous lives, in the third dimension, you lived as a monk abstaining from all worldly goods; as a serf badly beaten and abused by your master; as a sailor who sailed upon the open seas; and as a woman who sold her body for food. In this life you are attempting to deal with some of the issues raised by these other lives. If you think carefully, you will know what some of these issues are. "To the extent that you are able to confront and deal with them, you will aid your other alternate and multidimensional selves. In our reality, all those lives are ongoing now. In the third dimension, they are seen to be sequential. You may access information and help from your alternate personalities, if you wish. It is quite usual for you to meet them in your dream-state."

At this point, the Satron paused and an image of the wizened face of a bearded seaman appeared in Becka's consciousness. From the looks on the faces of the others, she felt that they, too, could see him.

The mariner seems tired, old, and ready to retire from work. Sitting on the deck of a schooner, looking out across the waters, he seems to be reflecting on his life. His thin face is lined and leathery; his body, wiry and sinewy. In his thoughts are images of women he has cared for and with whom he might have had an easier and better life if he had chosen differently. He is thinking of children who have disappeared from his life.

Now, as he prepares to begin yet another sea-journey, feelings of loneliness gnaw at him. His weariness is more than physical. It is spiritual. He is

Barbara Paul-Emile

reflecting on the good times when the camaraderie of his mates and the comfort of shared experiences more than made up for any losses he might have had. He remembers, also, those tough times when wrenching good-byes tempted him to make commitments. Unexpectedly, the man laughs out loud at the folly of his rêveries. He has had a better life than most, he is thinking; and with that, he gets up from his seat on the polished deck and goes back to working on the rigging. No recriminations. No remorse. His capacity for resilience is what carries him. He is a survivor.

As the mariner disappears from view, the lone figure of a scantily clad woman comes into focus. Walking slowly, smiling at the men who pass her by, her thigh-high skirt and hard, brassy face announce her vocation. The man who is living off her earnings had beaten her, the night before, for not bringing home enough. He considered her a slacker and an idler and had threatened to throw her out. The young woman's skin glistens pale in the neon light and she shivers, for the night is cold and there are no customers. There had been times she thought of killing herself but had lacked the courage. The clicking sound of her heels echoes as she wanders the desolate streets.

Stefan was mesmerized by the vignettes. He studied every detail intently. When he realized that all were tuned to his response, he appeared bemused and baffled, shrugged and appeared not to care. He did not share his thoughts. No one dared to probe either.

Before anyone could comment on the presentations, Joe-Joe spoke up. "Why are we looking at these," he said. "In what way do they help me?"

"Patience, patience," said the High Priestess. "You will see. You will see." She continued, "These beings represent lives that Stefan is leading in the *now*. He can draw on these experiences and learn from them, if he wishes. If he wishes to, he may also ignore them. In either case, they are all a part of who he is."

Stefan turned away and appeared unconvinced. He seemed anxious for the meeting to be over. Detaching himself from the group, he moved uncomfortably from one corner of the room to the other.

Jan spoke up in support of Joe-Joe's position and said, pointedly, "I can see where these entities reflect aspects of Stefan but I join Joe-Joe in asking what this means specifically for us?"

Becka understood the dynamics and felt that Jan was not anxious to learn from Stefan. The man was an anathema to him.

The Keeper ignored the open conflict between the two beings and, looking out through the walls, pointed to the spiral shaped trees growing in the mist-covered valley.

He explained, "Each spiral tree is connected to the other in ways seen and unseen. They grow from a common root. They communicate with each other and they support each other. Their twisted shape is representative of the spiraling double-helix in the

Barbara Paul-Emile

human DNA. As humans come into more of an understanding of oneness, these helices become aligned and are nourished by the great *Source*. You are all connected and must learn from each other."

The High Priestess, sensing that the seer was afraid to ask what she would know, walked over to her and said, "You do not always recall our meetings but we have conferred often in dream-time. I have never fully expressed my gratitude to you for coming to my aid when I worked with earth's ley lines during the spring ceremony of the goddess Gaia. The rains came and the land was fruitful for many years. You did well, Sister-Woman. Again my respects to you." And with that, she embraced Becka.

As the Priestess walked away, she smiled enigmatically and said to the assembly, "Becka fears we will not help with her mission. She thinks we have forgotten."

Turning to face the seer, Priestess Zalca continued, "No we have not forgotten, Sister-Woman. The Satron means to show that Joe-Joe's decision to return, or not, as the case might be, rides on key assumptions and issues that relate to us all. Much is taking place here on many levels."

"Now, young man, what say you?" the Priestess said smiling, facing Joe-Joe. "What is your will? You have heard us speak. The decision is yours. Do you wish to go back or not? What do you mean to do about the probability of continuing life as Joe-Joe in the first quarter of the twenty-first century?"

Chapter Fourteen

Seeding Realities

$\mathcal{J}$oe-Joe knew from the High Priestess' directness that it was time for him to come to a decision. He had to explain his intentions. Did he mean to return or to stay? As the time for decision drew closer, Becka grew edgy. She wished that the child would be more communicative and less hesitant. Why didn't he just come straight out and say what he wanted to do. Sensing Becka's impatience, Joe-Joe regarded her uneasily. The others, no less interested but probably less impatient, looked at him expectantly. Joe-Joe checked auras and scanned levels of energy fluctuations to see if he could read the group's appraisal of his dilemma.

Satisfied that he was receiving sufficient support, he said, "I have listened to you all and have heard you speak of your experiences and beliefs. I have tried to gain from the discussion, material that would be helpful to me in making my decision. I was

Barbara Paul-Emile

impressed by Jan's courage, Mosca's endurance, and the Priestess' power of discernment." He nodded and smiled at each entity in turn and continued, "The Satron is a light-being who did not incarnate as human. His vibrational frequency is higher than our own and his spectrum of reality broader. He cannot, therefore, be compared to us. From him I have learned about the nature of reality."

"Stefan is right," he said. "I will not return just so my father can live his life through me, or to prevent my mother grieving my loss. I love my parents, but I must find a way to create a worthwhile and productive life for myself. Yet, I find that I must reject Stefan's other views. His values are too dissimilar from my own. If I am to return to earth I must find a way to lead a life worth living."

Stefan, standing at the far corner of the room, laughed hoarsely and said, "You reject me, do you? Yet, you do exactly as I say. Didn't I tell you that life had to be lived for oneself alone? Didn't I say that?"

He looked away in mock disgust at what he considered pretense and hypocrisy.

Jan broke in and answered Stephan, "Yes, Joe-Joe wishes to live life for himself but not on your terms. Living for oneself does not mean that one cannot pursue worthwhile goals. Why live for mere self-gratification? Pursue a goal larger than yourself. Whatever it be."

Stefan regarded Jan with profound boredom as though to say, "I have responded to this argument before. Why bother?"

The High Priestess monitored the vibrations of both Stefan and Jan and decided that further debate between both entities would not advance the discussion. She turned the focus back to Joe-Joe by saying, "My son, what do you consider a life worth living?"

Joe-Joe smiled at her gratefully, bright color and highlights returning to his dream-body. He replied, "A life that is better than the one the Satron showed me that I am likely to live. Those lives were boring and uninteresting. I want to do worthwhile things. When I hear Mosca speak, I think of the legacy of slavery. When I hear Jan, I think of political oppression, which is still a factor in our world. Life must *mean* something." He continued somewhat idealistically, "I also want love and happiness in my life."

Stefan, although appearing bored, was paying close attention and evidently enjoying this part of the discussion. He smiled broadly and added, sardonically, "So now he wants love and happiness besides changing the world. What else? How about a little wealth?"

Joe-Joe was hurt by these cutting remarks and, turning to the Satron, said, "If Stefan is to interrupt me like this, I cannot continue. I have already said that I reject him and his views."

The Keeper gave a look to Stefan, which quieted him. The group returned its attention to Joe-Joe, who continued with more vigor than before, "If I

Barbara Paul-Emile

am to return to earth, I must see some alternate life plans. I want to see what else I can do with my life."

Turning to the Satron, he said, "You have made it plain that we are able to choose the life we wish to lead. Show me simulations so that I might choose." The Keeper said, "Your request is understandable and I will honor it. Let me repeat that *all* life paths are followed and developed, even those you do not choose. You are omni-directional. Your focus in the third dimension is so precise that you are not aware of the working out of alternate life paths in other dimensions."
There was silence as Joe-Joe considered the implications of the Satron's remarks.

The room darkened and the holographic insertions began. Details of landscape, sound and color developed to such a degree, that third dimensional reality is brought directly into the construct. Becka couldn't help wondering if such techniques could be used successfully on earth to seed realities. Who would know the difference? No one. Realities can be constructed. As the images progressed, Joe-Joe's early years are fast-forwarded and pass very quickly.

Joe-Joe emerges as a young man, a flamboyant figure, who develops a love for music and becomes a professional guitarist. His band, with the enigmatic name Vortex, is known for their cutting-edge, driving, mystical, and transcendental music. The group develops a strong local and international youth following and is being heavily marketed by the music industry.

Behind the driving rhythms of their hit songs, however, are lyrics that bring listeners into conscious awareness of the social and political manipulations that affect their lives. The band's music empowers and impulses people to access their inner ability to shape their own destinies. The powerful and hypnotic images of Joe-Joe singing, swaying, calling out to the audience, dancing to the music, enraptured by the emotional tie between his band and its audience, are compelling.

As a charismatic leader, Joe is courted by politicians who feel that his popularity can be used to support their own ends. Living on the edge as he does, he is seen as a politicized artist with dangerous social views and becomes the target for fanatics who feel that he should be eliminated. Several band members have been accused of using drugs, a common indictment against popular musicians given the culture in which they live. At least one unsuccessful attempt has been made on Joe's life and more might follow.

Vortex's music floods the room with its aggressive edge, echoing the bitter/sweetness of island life. Becka feels the power of the irresistible melodies move through her and is given to know that music is not trapped in any one dimension. Like ritual smoke, like chanting, singing, toning, the universal language of music breaks down all barriers and moves between worlds and between dimensions. Irrepressible,

Barbara Paul-Emile

uncontrollable, like air, like water, it flows endlessly increasing its vibration and frequency as it goes.

The Keeper explained that if the energy of the music is built on negativity and hostility, it empowers these feelings and moods. If built on love and joy, it enhances these emotions and can lead to redemption and inner healing on all levels of reality. Musical harmonies lift the spirit, release it and make it soar; or it can debase and entrap by lowering vibrational levels. Music, one of the most powerful of mediums, is mythic in scope and by nature.

Satron's comments are interrupted by the cessation of the melodies and the melding of the figures.

In the distance, Becka sees a large brownstone office complex. The exterior is imposing and reminds her of colonial government buildings in the island's capital. There are two soldiers keeping guard in front of the steep steps. Loud voices emanate from a large and well-appointed office. Seated at a desk is a young man, Joe-Joe, dressed semi-formally, wearing a linen Nehru jacket and matching beige pants. He is the picture of the scholarship boy who made good.

Sifting through papers on his desk, he fails to find the one he wants and, throwing the pile down in frustration, calls for his secretary. Another young man, Melvin, appears at the door. He is about the same age as Joe-Joe, only he is bespectacled and has an obsequious air about him. "Where are the listings of all the purchasing and sales transactions that have taken place this month?" demands Joe-Joe. "I distinctly asked that they be left on my desk."

"But I did, sir, I did," reiterates the young man, becoming agitated. "I placed the sheets with the tables there, myself, yesterday," he says, pointing to the desk.

"Well they aren't here, now." Joe-Joe responds, in a hard, tight voice. " Ask the director if he has them."

No sooner are the words spoken, than Mr. John Carstairs, known to the staff simply as Carly, enters the room. A stout man with a large ruddy face and fat neck, he walks in uninvited. The difference between the color of his exposed skin and that of his white shirt provides a startling contrast. Carly loves sports and spends his free hours sailing. He is always seeking to improve his tan. His ancestors have not been kind to him, however, for the pale complexion he has inherited does not tan easily. It merely turns turkey-red. Joe does not like the man and the feeling, evidently, is mutual. Carstairs asked Melvin to leave them alone. After the young man leaves the room, Carstairs closes the door and, standing with his back against it, stares steadily at Joe. In the silence, the air is fraught with anxiety.

Carly begins by saying, "Joe, I regret to say that a few days ago, while you were away, the Prime Minister ordered an audit. You were out of the country.

Barbara Paul-Emile

I did not think it necessary to contact you. The auditors spent the last few nights checking the books."

Joe stares blankly at him and says nothing.

The director continues, "Things do not look good. Your figures were not in order. In fact, there were significant discrepancies. I am afraid there will be need for further investigation. The assistant to one of the heads of our large companies, claims that you allowed them to reduce their tariffs while at the same time have private checks sent to your account. Of course, I believe none of these allegations, but the man was adamant, having kept his own private records. You know how these petty officials are. The Prime Minister has to investigate. Elections are not so far off. You know what all that means."

He screws up his face in mock annoyance, while pausing just long enough to let the implications of his accusation sink in. Joe listens quietly, he knows that his every reaction is being monitored.

When Carly ends, Joe says, calmly, "Is this why my papers were removed?"

"As I said, old boy, what could we do?" Carstairs continues, his eyes widening in mock innocence. "You were not here ..."

Joe knows just how much he is enjoying this. Carly has wanted his job for a long time. This was his chance. Joe picks up the phone and says to Melvin, "See if the Prime Minister is in his office."

Carly said in as helpful a tone he could muster, "Sorry, you will not be able to reach him. It will be impossible for him to meet or speak with you until this whole thing blows over. Would not appear well if he did, you know."

Joe knows what Carly is thinking, but the man is wrong. He would not roll over and play dead. Neither would he fall on his knees. He has made some dicey decisions. Yes. He has taken gifts, now and then, as everyone else did, but he knows that his papers are in order. This is a trap out of which he would have to fight his way.

Joe hears himself saying, coolly, "Thank you, John for letting me know what happened in my absence. I understand, the Prime Minister's position. But I know that when the smoke clears, I will be vindicated. My papers are in order."

"Just as I thought old man," said John amiably. "Just as I thought. Shall I ring for your car?"

What power Joe-Joe wields, thought Becka. But what the hell has he gotten himself into now? It looked really serious. What kind of friends was he keeping? An image of the Prime Minister had appeared the first time he was referred to by Joe-Joe, revealing him to be a crafty, wily politician who had risen up from the people but who had done little else but make sure he lined his own pockets. Was Joe to be his scapegoat?

Joe-Joe looked at the images and was perplexed. He did not ask to see how the situation was resolved. The scene shifted to show him as a child

Barbara Paul-Emile

sitting atop a fence, whistling to himself.

Joe-Joe, along with other children, is on an excursion with their teacher to a local field to wait for the wild flowers, known locally as "four-o'clocks" because they open their buds at evening. The teacher says it is almost time, and the children watch and wait, as, slowly, the pink bell-shaped open to reveal the delicate flower.

Joe is a country boy and he has seen this unfolding take place many times and is no longer impressed. He does not care to string the flowers on long grass stalks as do the other children. He had come only because of his admiration and affection for his teacher, Miss Hines. He has already decided to be a teacher, just like her. He wants to be as well-educated as she is and be looked up to by the community. When he walks down the road, he wants everyone to say, "Good morning and Good evening teacher" and show their respect as he walks by. Joe always sits in the front of the class and doesn't mind being regarded as Miss Hines' favorite.

The child grows and ages to reveal a graying, middle-aged man. Portly in size, stern and forbidding, he is principal of a school. The pupils fear but do not love him. In accepting the headmastership, he has reached the pinnacle of his career. Life's intangible rewards have, however, eluded him. He finds his professional activities dull and predictable.

In fact, he is having a secret affair with one of the teachers in his school and has been forced, through circumstances, to finance two clandestine abortions. A good citizen, he sings in the church choir on Sundays and is envied by the community for his successful life.

As the characters crinkled, folded, and disappeared, Becka continued to stare through the transparent walls of the retreat. "What will Joe choose to do?" she wondered. To her way of thinking, these life-lines were a mixed bag. "Still, at least he has choices," she thought. Improvement was always possible.

The shaman ran through the preview of the lives repeatedly, reflected on them, and decided to withhold judgment. This group seemed to function as well in silence as in debate, Becka observed to herself. She suspected that some level of communication was going on, even though it was unacknowledged. Sometimes, she felt that thoughts from the others swam into her consciousness. At other times, she felt that she was directing ideas to them. She did not quite know how the process worked, so she decided to watch and wait.

Stefan, who felt free to offer comments on all subjects, whether invited to or not, said, with much amusement, "I think those were particularly interesting lives. A good mix: sex, boredom and larceny, set to music. Of course, let us not forget a few drugs to smooth the way. I especially liked the politician's and the headmaster's lives. These were truly excellent. I am glad to see that nothing has changed - a little corruption, a little veniality, and a lot of fornication. Life as usual! I forecast a small turn in prison or at least bankruptcy, dismissal in disgrace and/or an untimely death."

He laughed cynically and beamed brightly at his fellows.

Everyone ignored him except Joe-Joe who, looking miserably at the Satron, said, "Stefan has no right to make these remarks about my choices. Who is he to comment?"

The Satron replied, "Think, child. You commented on his choices. You showed your disapproval. He should be free to comment on your choices."

"Why? What gives him the right?" demanded Joe-Joe, becoming more belligerent.

"Because he is a part of you. He is a part of us all. In fact, he *is* you," said the Satron.

There was silence.

"How can he be me, I don't even know him," Joe-Joe blurted out, completely disregarding the deeper significance of Satron's remarks.

The Keeper looked at the boy compassionately and said "Joe-Joe, I can understand your feelings. But I must tell you this. You cannot reject Stefan. He is a part of you. He *is* you."

Joe-Joe, who was simply annoyed at first, was becoming more and more irritated. "How can he be me. I am not like him. There is nothing in common between us."

Mosca, who had remained silent during most of the proceedings, roused himself and said, "Why insult the boy in this way?"

Jan shook his head, frowned and looked in disbelief at the Satron. His stare said, "What are you saying? You're making a mistake."

Stefan, feeling that he understood the import of the Satron's remarks well enough, raised his eyebrows, beamed, and chuckled to himself. Things were looking up, getting better and better. Now the Satron was on *his* side for a change. He was enjoying the assembly's discomfort and startled reaction.

The sea-merchant preened himself in the spotlight. This time he felt he had the upper hand. He relished being the center of attention and having the Satron promote his interests. Of course, he had no idea what the Keeper meant by his obscure remarks. But who cared? Nobody here was better than he was.

You, Mosca, struggle with the implications of lost freedom. You, Jan, work out the high cost of personal liberty.

You, Becka, have undertaken a perilous journey in the name of love in order to help another choose a more enriching life.

You, Stefan, work on the shadow side of life - the denial of feelings, the abuse of others, the taking, the hoarding of useless material substances - to fill the empty spaces in your unfulfilled life.

You, Joe-Joe, have left a life you felt would be non-productive to explore ways to construct a life that offers you more opportunities.

"Along with other questions, all of you deal with the meaning of death. You are each within the other. You are multidimensional beings. The hatred you feel for another, you feel for yourself. The love you feel for another, you feel for yourself. Beloveds, you must come to terms with this. That is why we are here."

The atmosphere in the Satron's architectural construct became radiant. Light particles floated and oscillated in the air. The entities found themselves surrounded by floating geometric shapes and designs such as they had never seen before. As the sacred forms disappeared, a vortex began to form in the center of the room. The air became compressed and rotated in a circular motion. Becka felt her consciousness expanding as the circles grew larger. There was a magnetic pull to the center of the vortex that drew all

Chapter Fifteen

Apotheosis

𝒯he lights in the Satron's broad auric field shimmered and pulsed as he observed the group members. He read and registered the bewildered responses of several entities.

After a time, he addressed them all by saying, "Some of you here share Joe's feelings. You accept some entities here and reject others. You love some and loathe others. I must now tell you that you are all *one*. Every single entity here is a part of a whole. You are like facets of a single diamond. A single brilliant diamond. You each reflect the light and the shadow that each other brings. You are multidimensional beings. You are all things at once. Together, all of you form one single being.

"Unfortunately, all of you except the High Priestess have forgotten. You no longer remember your true identity. You have lived many probable lives and have been different beings with different personality structures, experiencing different qualities of life. In some instances, your lives have reflected virtue and honor; in others, you have courted materiality and have been shallow and corrupt. You have always learned from your experiences and have transmitted the essence of your lessons to the whole. As I regard you all, I am filled with deep compassionate feelings. "

There was a stunned silence.

Jan spoke up, disbelievingly, "How can all of us be *one*? What does being *one* mean? And how, in the name of everything that is good, can I be one with a being who traffics in human life. One who makes a living off the destruction of others? I will not believe this."

Jan was willing to accept Stephan as an entity, a man, to whom life was given and who, to his way of thinking, had trivialized it and was using it unwisely. This was the only connection and one about which one need not boast. Nothing more.

Mosca cursed under his breath and, looking at the Satron, said, "Tell us another tale, old man, if you will, but not this one. I will not conspire with you to reconstruct this monster. Stefan should not live."

The Satron said, "Remember, what I said to you: there is no death. Even if Stefan did not return to his physical body, he would live on in all of you. Mosca, this knowledge was known and held sacred and secret by your elders for eons. If you access your ancestral memory, all will return to you."

Jan interjected, "We do not only take, we attempt to give back. We fight and, if necessary, die for liberty. What is he willing to die for? He lives to subjugate and destroy others in order to create wealth for himself at any cost. What can we have in common?"

The High Priestess said, "It is time that you all be fully awakened from your sleep. Study the many vignettes offered you. Think about them. Seek the meaning behind them. Your present life is just one such a dramatic portrayal. Your story has as much validity and significance as do the others, not more. Others can observe your life as you observe theirs. There is communication between the actors of each drama."

The Priestess paused and looked silently at the gathering. No one spoke. All searched their mental files to recall the variety of holographic images they had seen.

The Priestess pressed on: "All of our live together form a complex mosaic, a prism. The larg pattern of all our lives shows a search for the meani of liberty, freedom, and a search for human dignity worth. Beneath his cruel and selfish actions, St also searches for his truest self. He must find w himself the courage to reject the values of consciousness and follow a higher road. All of y the tug of his struggle.

"You may accept his actions or reje But each one of us will respond to them.

into its center. While most resisted, the Priestess moved right into the heart of it.

One by one, each member of the group felt drawn into the whirling current. Becka felt the intensity of the pull and gave way. There was nothing else to do. She could not resist the swirling movement of the energy. Everything happened so quickly. Her conventional mind, against which she tested all phenomena, had fled. She could not fault it for negligence. In this dimension, its effectiveness, was in abeyance. It had no significant role to play. The seer let go and allowed her consciousness freedom to find its medium.

Becka feels herself spinning, spinning until she loses awareness. When she knows herself again, she has no light-body and no dream-body. There is no auric field around her. She is pure consciousness. All astral levels have been peeled away and she is her essential self. She feels lighter, freer than she has ever felt before, for she has released all density. The dreamwalker allows this experience to sink in and begins to explore her surroundings. Nestled next to her are other consciousnesses. One issues forth a smooth, harmonic vibration that is strength-giving and comforting. Becka senses the resonance of the High Priestess.

Next, there is Joe-Joe's consciousness, searching and adventuresome, huddled close to that of Mosca and Jan. All three pulse together rhythmically.

Vibrating alone is Stefan. His pulsing is erratic and his frequency faint and weak as though it is farthest from the center. Becka reaches out to him. Suddenly, there is a spontaneous implosion and the dreamwalker feels her borders give way as an even deeper bonding and merging takes place between their consciousness. All separations dissolve and all emissions become one. There is no periphery, no center. Each is sublimated into something larger than itself.

Intoxicating sensations flood Becka's aware-ness with feelings of rapture and delight. She feels colossal, powerful, grand beyond belief. Emanating from unknown sources are feelings of bliss, harmony and love. She floats in a sea of rich colors that dance around her only to change into musical harmonies that resonate through her. The feeling is thrilling, erotic, celestial. Becka feels herself growing larger and larger as her antennae open to the galaxy. Her awareness dances in spiral waves, spinning in and then out again and back in on itself. Strange flickering lights of vibrant luminosity spin round. She has the sensation of being wrapped or cocooned in streams of pulsing light filaments.

The dreamwalker senses the presence of another, but what or whom she doesn't know. She is well aware that her companions are with her. She senses them all. Only, now, they share a larger identity. They are parts of a greater whole. All have, indeed, become one. Yet, within this great confluence of energy, Becka knows that each essence maintains its own flawless integrity. Each entity maintains pinpoint awareness of his or her own self and of each other. Jan is Jan, Stefan is Stefan. She is herself, as are all the others.

As the seer contemplates these extraordinary circumstances, a soft pink light begins to spread through the area of their containment. Its source is unknown, but it starts with one awareness and spreads to another, and another, and another... Becka feels herself touched by this light. Instantaneously, she knows, along with the others, where they are.

*They are within the Light-Keeper. They are within the Satron. They **are** the Satron. He is their Oversoul. As her consciousness expands, Becka perceives that she is surrounded by rivers of resplendent light, which stretch out in all directions. Encompassing these streams of light are larger circles of even greater intensity. Their brilliance, luminosity and radiance seem limitless.*

There is no need for thought or temporal understanding. There is nothing to strive for and nothing to achieve. All simply is. In acceptance, each being experiences its higher self. The seer feels herself lifted to dimensions where love vibrations are the essence of all relationships and interactions. She and her companions rest in this state of unrestrained joy and peace for a period undefined by mortal time. Slowly the light withdraws and Becka feels herself falling. Little by little density returns and, gradually, her dream-body reshapes itself.

Once again Becka found herself in the construct, on the planet with the twin suns. Her heart-center, joyous and ecstatic, could not hold her feelings. It overflowed into words and images:

Streams of light filaments rising, falling
Pulsing, flowing over all
Consuming all, becoming all
Changing into oneness.

Resonating harmonies, colors, sounds
Forms, glittering shapes
Chords, dancing, merging, melding
Whirling, spiraling vortices.

Beauty, power, shimmering grace
Radiance, luminously bright
Traversing galaxies without end
Opening closing and opening again
Resplendence, joy, ecstasy.

The multidimensional beings reassembled and regarded each other with awe and reverence. The feelings of love, generated and fostered among them during the soul-merge, clung to them as a noctilucent cloak, and the light filaments in their aura shimmered and glowed with soft colors. The air was infused with fragrances, sweet and subtle, and with the soft strains of distant harmonies. As though to hold on to the shared experience, no one spoke.

Breaking the silence, the Satron said, "You have experienced your larger identity. You now know yourself to be part of me as I am a part of each of you. You are fragments of my being. An American philosopher, used the term "Oversoul" aptly, to describe a higher union of spirit that transcends polarities and is beyond surface differences.

"As part of a larger whole, you choose the life you wish to lead in order to gather experiences for all. You grow as a result of these experiences. Your ultimate goal is to choose the light under all circumstances; and to know yourself in the third dimension, for who you really are: multidimensional light-beings. You are *one*, regardless of the historical time in which you dwell, your country, ethnicity, or the level of light you wish to radiate. There is no separation between you."

He continued, "You are a *family of light*. You are one with each other and with me, as I am one with all other Light-Keepers and their fragmented selves. I, also, am a part of a larger entity, and that entity a part of a larger, and a larger ... And so it is.

There is no separation in creation. There never was. All humans are light-beings. You assign yourself learning tasks and set about completing them. To handicap your course, you have decided to forget who you truly are, so as to find your way to the light again. But, always, your essence rests with me. This is probably the ultimate mystery. For you must return again to a place you have never left. This is sometimes called 'the journey without distance'." With that, he laughed softly and fell silent.

Then Jan, his aura resplendent, spoke up: "In what ways do we help and nourish each other?" he asked.

Zalca, the High Priestess, responded, "You Jan, and also Mosca, struggle to come to terms with the very elements Stefan has allowed to become central to his life: the *deprivation of liberty*, both private and public. Stefan has not allowed himself to feel for others. Neither does he think much about the welfare of others. While it is healthy to love and honor the self, this should not be accomplished at the expense of your fellows. By this I mean you must not place boulders in the path of others, so as to 'smooth' your own progress. Stefan has to learn that he shares with all of you and, if he wishes, can access your learning and transform his life. You are each free to change your own reality."

Mosca, his dream-body translucent and countenance serene, spoke, and as he did, his heart center pulsed. "Stefan must learn from this experience, the meaning of union," he said. "He must know that he stands bound with me and cannot be free until he honors my freedom. I live within him and he within me. He must free himself to feel my loss. Only then will he find his true self. I am beginning to understand the connection between all of life and I will seek to honor that connection."

Everyone waited to hear from Stefan, whose

Barbara Paul-Emile

vibration rate had visibly quickened as a result of the exaltation. At first, he hesitated to share his feelings. There was an observable air of newness and wonder about him. Acquiescing to their request, he addressed his light-family: "This experience is new to me. I do not fully understand it. But I feel that I am not as alone as I once was. I must allow myself to feel ... I sensed all your essences within myself. All your traits lie within me, I feel them. I can access your experiences. I can rely on your knowledge within me ... I will not close my eyes to pain ... I ..." Stephan's comments disjointed and stumbling reflected the new truths he struggled to absorb. He felt enfolded in the radiance of the group and the warmth of it both surprised and nourished him.

The mood was one of joy, for all knew that the sea-merchant had spoken well. When he beheld the response to his halting declaration, the vibrancy of his etheric field increased and Stefan began to feel free. For the first time, he accessed the oneness ...

Satron drew the light-beings, once again, into himself and then gently released them. In Satron's release, however, Becka and the others felt the Keeper's pain. Observing them, he transmitted the following message in images and tones that echoed his mood unmistakably: "Your desires and intentions are clear. But know, that in the third dimension, density increases and many of you will feel cut off from me and from this reality. It is then that the testing comes. Can you attune yourself to what you truly know deep within? Can you through meditation and contemplation, or through any other means, creative endeavors and the like, call back into consciousness what you know and have agreed to do? For the amnesic effect on earth is strong, as are the social pressures. You will be free to tune out your dreamtime experiences if you choose. Remember that the others and I remain within each one of you as impulses and as intuitive feelings. You are dearly loved and you are never alone."

At the Satron's words, the love vibration increased so strongly in the room that it triggered the encoding of oneness implanted in each entity. Feelings of unconditional love and infinite caring flowed through the group to such a degree, that members pledged within themselves never to disappoint the Light-Keeper, or each other, but to remember ... to remember ... to remember.

The Light-Keeper, speaking to all, yet to each singly, said:

> *In third density, you must*
> *Cherish the self I gave you*
> *Listen to your breathing*
> *Hear the pauses between your words*
> *Notice the movement of the body.*
>
> *Lay your conscious mind aside*
> *Become filled with my knowing*
> *My being, the elixir of Spirit*

Feel your connectedness to all things.

See the vistas open to you
Value your dreams, your desires
No one can give the rewards
You must give to the self.

No one can honor self but self
For you're one aspect of a prism
Crystal, bright, eternal
Feel the light refract through you.

Chapter Sixteen

The Family of Light

$\mathcal{B}$ecka remembered the sweet sensations of the submergence. She remembered the connectedness, the feeling of oneness and the immense joy of being part of a larger whole. She understood herself and her relationships differently, and had a deeper understanding of the implications of her journey. Initially, she had thought Joe-Joe's decision an easy one. Now, she had a greater appreciation for the layering of realities and of the nature of multidimensionality.

Never again could she conceive of herself as being alone, for within her consciousness she would always hear the echoes of the others. Her threshold of awareness had been raised and, while the knowledge of her true identity could be covered up, it could never be lost. All of her multidimensional selves could sense her thoughts and impulses as she did theirs and, if they chose to, they could be open to learning from each other.

In that convergence of spirits that she had experienced, the seer knew herself to be both singular and plural: both herself and others. In expressing her identity, she could truthfully say, "We are Becka. We are the collective." The immensity of this understanding baffled the lower mind. She had been transformed and so had her perception of everything. The shaman smiled at the thought, for now she was free to access the others, not only in times of need, but simply to enjoy their companionship. She could do all these things if she maintained clear channels. Becka savored this new sense of being.

The Satron monitored his many selves. Each one was lost in private contemplation. Their thoughts filtered into his consciousness. The revelation of their true identity affected each of them differently. Mosca pondered the concept of the *oneness of all*. He puzzled over the inference that Stefan's weakness was also within himself. Stefan's impulse, which led to his egregious actions, were also within him. Then he considered the significance of the High Priestess' gift to him of her insignia: the hawk. It was a bird he had always admired. Sleek and black, it flew high. He would always treasure this gift. He drew strength from this talisman given to him by his Sister-Woman.

Jan had left the group and reduced himself to his essence: a ball of light. Floating upward, he settled atop the structure where it opened to the suns. He was lost in thought. Death, he surmised, might well be like the great merging where one returned to the source. Earthly conception of annihilation might be faulty. After all, death was only a leaving of the physical body. Knowledge of his true identity filled him with joy and with a profound sense of peace. It was reassuring to remember that, during the great merging of his many selves with the Satron, he had not lost sense of his own individual integrity. His personality-self remained inviolate. He was Jan. He always knew himself.

As he considered these matters, Jan was inspired by the Satron to know that nothing was ever lost - no personality, or being, or thought - so great, so magnificent, so multi-layered was this universe with its dimensions without number. The enlightened ones know that animals considered extinct have merely left this dimension for another. That is all. Nothing is ever lost. Jan's mind buckled under the weight of this awareness. Then, inexplicably, he smiled, for he was relieved to remember that, in his identity as the Keeper, he could access and integrate greater and greater levels of knowledge. He was a part of All-that-is.

Joe stood alone listening to the music that floated through the landscape, carried by molecules of air. The light-entities could, by their thought processes, augment the melodies for their own private pleasure. Becka noticed that Joe-Joe, the child, had increased in age and stature. Now, he presented himself as a man in his early twenties wearing casual clothing: jeans and

Barbara Paul-Emile

sports shirt. He appeared relaxed and at ease with himself.

Under the guidance of the Keeper, he had come to understand why, in his life-plans, he had chosen this moment to consider whether or not to continue living on earth. Joe understood that he had approached a growth portal which, because it materialized for him, had materialized for his multidimensional selves, and the Satron as well. He knew that all would be affected by his decision in far-reaching ways. In entering this portal, he had answered *the call* and begun *the journey*. In doing so, he had challenged all of his alternate selves to move ahead in their search for a larger identity.

Joe weighed and sifted the lessons offered to him. He contemplated the nature of his choices and then made his decision. He wanted to share his choice with his light-family. Calling the group together, he focused his immediate attention on Becka; this woman who had journeyed into the unknown to find him and to bring him back to earth. She had shown courage, bravery and a capacity to give of herself for the good of others. In undertaking this night journey, she had harnessed the archetypal energies of the *warrior, the seeker and the seer.* In her search for him, she had been forced to face the unknown, releasing much of what she thought she knew. But in finding him, she had found herself.

He shared his heart-energy with her in gratitude. She sat before him, her auric colors ablaze with the fire of her adventurous spirit and her features radiant with her new sense of self. Joe honored her by addressing his first remarks to her.

He said, "Yes, I am willing to return to earth. I will return to my home, to my family and to my friends. I will create a new reality."

The relief in the room was palpable. Although Joe's multidimensional selves had sensed the drift of his thoughts, no one had tried to access his decision prematurely, out of respect for his free will. This announcement was his to make.

Joe continued, "I choose to devote myself to the arts as a way of bringing fulfillment to myself and to others. I, therefore, choose the life of the musical artist, singer and band-leader. I will access traits from all of you, my light-family, to enrich my life."

Again, there was silence, as everyone waited to know how Joe would create the particular aspects of the life he had chosen. With increased confidence, Joe-Joe continued:

"From Becka, seer, adventurer and guide,
I choose love, daring and the spirit of the quest;

From brave Mosca,
I take inner discipline, fortitude, endurance and courage;

From the indomitable Jan,

I select faith and commitment to those freedoms
on which life depends;

From Stefan, light-seeker,
I learn the true value of things: from his
choices, I affirm my commitment to continued
growth and change;

From High Priestess Zalca, the life-stream of
her people,
I learn the rights and responsibilities of power;

From Satron, Light-Keeper, who holds us
within himself,
I learn oneness and the essential unity of all
life;

From all my alternate selves,
I learn that there are but two main attributes:
love and fear.
I have chosen love and I have chosen life. "

Becka noticed that the vegetation in the
environment showed increased sensitivity to energy
fluctuations and was responding to the increased light
vibration and to the higher frequencies emanating from
the entities. The spectrum of colors reflected in the
foliage showed change, and leaves and stems glistened
with heightened color. A thin mist of crystal droplets
swept across the surface of the ground as with a

painter's brush. The air, sweet and fragrant, blew in great gusts across the enchanted landscape. Musical harmonies, faintly heard in the distance, increased in volume.

A light-form was seen on the distant horizon, approaching the complex. The group tracked its advance and watched with interest as it materialized in the room. A being, manifesting as female, approached first Satron and then Joe. Her unbounded aura filled the room. It was transmitted to all present that this was an entity, yet unborn, who was readying herself for entry into earth. Presently, she was creating her life choices and writing her story. The Satron made the entity welcome and smiled knowingly at Joe who had risen to greet her.

As Joe and the visitor faced each other, the shades of their auras blended into a rainbow of colors. Their frequencies vibrated together, and their etheric lights pulsed rhythmically. The two beings had established a feeling of harmony and balance between them that indicated a deep resonance and a commonality of purpose.

The multidimensional selves watched with pleasure as the entities merged and then withdrew from each other. Joe's decision to return to earth - that message had been carried across the galaxy - and in response, this light-being, intending to incarnate, had offered to join his journey.

High Priestess Zalca approached the couple and, demonstrating her extraordinary powers, created a hologram in which they saw themselves wrapped in garlands of flowers. So vivid was the re-creation, that the fragrance of the blossoms filled the room. Satron manifested wine and the Priestess danced for the couple in celebration of the marriage yet to be. She danced the ritual dance of bonding and of consecration. Her movements graceful, sensual, and enchanting, increased the love vibration already elevated in the room.

As the strains of the music died away, everyone embraced the couple. The bonding was complete. Satron transmitted to his alternate selves his joy at this union, which signified the ultimate oneness of all, and his own great pleasure at the choices these two entities had made. Swiftly, Gloria, as the entity would be called upon its entry into earth, began to shapeshift and return to her essence: a blue and white ball of dazzling light. Becka watched as, with quick darting movements, she circled the room and flew towards the horizon.

The Satron looked about him at the shining fragments of himself and said, "Some of you have asked to glimpse aspects of other entities whose lives parallel your own. I will be brief, for third density earth is still subject to time."

Becka felt her inner screen cloud over and then clear.

A military officer is crouching in the bush holding a rifle in his gloved hand. He wears army fatigues and is leading a small company of men, all pale skinned with brown or blond hair and blue or light-brown eyes. The clothes they wear, heavy and dark, offer camouflage while protecting them against the bitter cold.

Their patrol company has been ambushed by a larger enemy force. Two of their best men, seeking a way out, have already been hit by sniper fire. Out there in the darkness, the commander knows that their movements are being monitored by their would-be captors, armed with infrared weapons. The enemy will wait until morning before mounting the assault, so sure are they in their belief that their prey is trapped.

The company is tense and strained, but each man is a seasoned veteran and will not give way to fear. Believing in their leader's skill and in his knowledge of the terrain, they feel sure that he will outwit the attackers and allow for their escape. The officer can feel the confidence his men have in him and gives thanks that he studied the terrain well before setting out. The land is hilly and precipitous, full of hidden gorges and small ravines, and covered by scattered patches of thick vegetation.

As the leader lays still in the silence scanning the mountainside, he recalls a dream he had the night before in which a figure, whose face he could not see, showed him a trapped creature being freed and another larger animal running in a sunny meadow. The identity of the entity was not revealed to him. Moving cautiously, he and his men slip away under

Barbara Paul-Emile

cover of darkness, into the secret gorge between the steep cliffs, and are gone before daybreak ...

The figures meld and the scene fades ...

Now, Becka sees thousands of people standing in a field. The climate is hot and the vegetation is rich and lush. Heat rises in streams of vapor that shimmer in the moist air. The seer struggles to identify the region. As the figures became clearer, she sees in the distance a man robed in ceremonial garments, standing atop a mound. The people watch in silence.

Suddenly, out of the skies, comes a powerful roaring, rushing sound that reverberates off the heights of the mountain and resonates across the valley. The glistening, flashing lights, the whirling winds frighten the assembly and they kneel in awe. The transport descends, resplendent with its shimmering wheels and glistening armor. The light emitted from the chariot shines so brightly that the populace is temporarily blinded by the brilliance.

The vehicle comes to rest before the man. Two chimeras, part animal/part angel, emerge as his escorts. The regal figure bids farewell to his people and blesses them. As he enters the Merkabah, involuntarily, his people cry out at their loss. As he takes the reigns of his light-chariot in his hands, they fall silent.

Slowly, the celestial vehicle rises higher and higher above the ground. Energy bands of silver and gold dance around it. The Merkabah is dazzling in its beauty. The craft hovers, then slowly, ever so slowly, begins its ascent. The people gaze on it, fearfully and in awe, until it disappears into the clouds and is gone from sight. Only the harmony of sounds produced by its soaring propulsion lingers in the air.

The people cry out again and their cry became a wail, "Our king and prophet, Anuk, has ascended. He who had blessed the crops and enriched the land. He who had led us in the right path. He has left us. He has ascended."

Then, Prince Nubar, the anointed successor, steps forward, his face moist with tears. Turning his eyes to the skies, he cries:

Anuk!
King and Prophet of the Gods
Do not forget your people
Do not forget your sanctuary.

Our lights will burn in memory
At the fullness of the moon
At the rising of the sun
At the offering of the grain
At the coming of the rains
We will honor you.

Anuk, Anuk,
Prophet and King.

So great is the outpouring of spirit on this day,

Barbara Paul-Emile

that the spectacle would pass into legend. Many would recall that the sick and the crippled were healed that day and unbelievers converted.

The temple priestesses dance the sacred dance and sing:

> *Anuk, Anuk*
> *King and Prophet*
> *Left the earth*
> *A Light-being*
> *He'll never know death*
> *He'll return at birth*
> *Anuk, our guardian*
> *Forever.*

An involuntary contraction passed through Becka's dream-body as the significance of what she had witnessed entered her consciousness. She had witnessed an ascension. Who was this man, this king, this prophet, this entity? Somehow the life-force was familiar to her.

In silence, each entity searched for the meaning of this latest demonstration. Their circle of connections kept growing ever wider. The Satron impulsed the collective to know that they and their alternate selves had played many different roles in many lives—the murdered and the murderer; the conquered and the conqueror; the healed and the healer; the rich man and the beggar; the priest and the sinner. All were required to experience life as the *'other.'*

The Keeper responded to their thought-questions by saying, "Now that you are aware of your alternate selves and their parallel lives, they will visit you. The channels have been opened. Understanding is all. In the planning of each incarnation, you make a determination as to your polarization, whether it will be male or female. Entities choose their ethnic, national and gender grouping in light of the lessons to be learned and the dramas to be experienced. Remember, all time is one and all lives are happening in the *now*."

The multidimensional selves knew that the time for leave-taking was at hand. Dreamtime must come to an end. Some entities sought private audiences with their peers, while others wandered off alone. Looking about the room, Becka noticed that Mosca and Stefan had left the structure and floated out over the uneven ground. They were deep in conversation with each other.

With the aid of charts, maps and holograms, the High Priestess taught Joe to channel the earth's energy through the chakra systems of the body. She explained the use of these subtle frequencies in the creation of music. To Becka, the seer, Zalca explained the use of touch along the meridian lines of the body as a powerful healing modality.

Jan, who had the toughest part of his journey ahead of him, spent much time with the Keeper. At different points in their conversation energy exchanges took place between them and their auras merged into

Barbara Paul-Emile

pulsing spiral forms of light. Becka watched with fascination as Jan's magnetic field widened and brightened until it extended hundreds of feet in radius beyond the complex.

As the twin red suns dimmed, this special gathering of Satron's light-family all prepared to end their dream-time and return to third dimension. A somber mood settled over the landscape. No one wanted to be the first to leave. Parting, or even the semblance of it, is ever difficult. Becka noticed that the shadings of the vegetation and the environment had paled and a gray pall settled over the landscape.

Stefan, drawing from the feeling of oneness in the room, said, "I feel the pain of this parting. We must not forget that we will not be alone. We are within each other and will have access to each other. This is not the end."

Satron, added, "You will now return to your separate centuries and countries and personal circumstances. But before you depart, I will give each of you a gift."

The Satron called Mosca to him and to the delight of his alternate selves merged with the Yoruba warrior and together they formed a glorious light-entity. As the African returned to form, the Keeper said:

"To you, Mosca,
I give the gift of freedom and discovery;
You will find what you thought was lost to you.

To you, Stefan,
I give the gift of internal strength to withstand
the urgings of social consciousness and the will
to follow your own higher self.

To you, Becka,
I give the gift of healing and of memory;
Upon your return, you will have full recall of
all that has taken place.

To you, High Priestess,
I give the ability to appear to your people after
you have left to remind them of their purpose
and their great destiny.

To you, Joe,
I give the will to lead a fulfilling life that
honors the value you have chosen as important
to yourself.

To you, Jan,
I give a peaceful translation. Your sacrifice will
never be forgotten and your legacy will be the
gift of liberty to your nation."

Again, the Keeper gathered all his selves to him
and loved them. As the entities emerged from the
oneness, each became a fire-ball of light that took
to the air and floated into deep space. Satron,

Barbara Paul-Emile

Light-Being, looked across the horizon and saw six balls of light shimmering in the color streams of Andromeda. He sent them love and increased light-energy to increase their resplendence. He watched as they transformed themselves into flashing bursts of light.

Within himself, Satron could hear their voyaging sounds as they streaked across the galaxy. With his inner vision, he monitored their course and saw them flying in chevron formation, led by Jan, followed on the right by the High Priestess, Stefan and Mosca, and on the left by Becka and Joe. Realizing that the addition of one more entity on the left would complete their pattern, the Keeper joined them. When the group saw his approach, they sounded out their joy, increased their colorful auras and drew him into their magnetic fields.

The harmonics of the collective reverberated among the stars, across the spheres and penetrated the outer reaches of the galaxies. By desire, all entities melded together and became a dazzling ball of phosphorescent fire. As a single being, they trans-mitted their signature- identity deep into space. Their message, expressed in a single note of high tonal quality rang out, *"We are one. We are one. All is well."* This broadcast echoed through the immensity of space as they flashed through the darkness of the void. Their wholeness was their song:

HEARTSONG

One spirit are we, one heart
Separate, yet together
In oneness, yet apart
Sing we our heart-song to the stars.

Arching through spaces infinite
Anchored in the corridors of time
We are love, we are light
We are light-travelers
We are One.

Barbara Paul-Emile

Chapter Seventeen

Rebirth

*A*fter the long night, Becka felt her spirit re-enter her body with a soft thud. She opened her eyes to see Joe-Joe's guardian spirits retreat into the unseen world. The calling of these golden ones is to serve. Gladly would they accompany him on his new journey. The guides knew that the boy had made his decision and would live the life he had chosen. Joe-Joe's vital signs appeared to be stronger. His breathing was deep and regular and his face had a soft glow, as he lay asleep. The shaman knew that his recovery would be quick.

Becka's own guardians waited expectantly for her to make her intentions clear. Did she mean to stay in body or return to astral traveling? They sensed her ambivalence. The house was quiet. The crowing of the rooster had not yet heralded the coming of day. Becka remained in a light trance. She maintained her connection with her multidimensional selves and recognized their individual signature vibrations. Accessing the Keeper's gift, the shaman decided to return to the astral level. She felt drawn back for she had unfinished business there. Gently, the obeah woman centered her focus and released her consciousness from her body. Re-entry was easy.

The shaman follows Jan's signals. He has awakened in his cell from what he thought was an uneasy sleep and is experiencing some difficulty keeping his consciousness in his body. Fragments of dreams filled with strange images and shrouded figures drift in and out of his still blurred mental vision. Representations of dream-scenes keep approaching the edges of his consciousness and retreating, float away.

The prisoner feels that he has been flying through colored skies among shimmering particles of light. Blisteringly bright figures whose faces he can not quite see hover around him. He has faint memories of strangely shaped leaves and falling water. The rest is unclear. Yet, for all the busyness of his dreaming, Jan has an extraordinary sense of peace. The anger and anxiety that had plagued him are gone. The contemplation of his own death is no longer as frightening as he had feared. Inexplicably, lines from a favorite poem surface in his mind:

> *I will leave this old and empty castle*
> *I will lay my weapons down*

I will walk across the portal
I will take the road to town.

The sun beats on my shoulders
Earth shakes 'neath my feet
No armor will I carry
No weapons do I need.

For I will take my freedom
Taste the fruits of my new joys
Feel the breezes brush my lyre
Hear the music of the stars.

I will honor my own journey
Finding peace in my own way.

Jan refuses food this morning and elects instead to spend time in meditation. During these moments of quietness, dream sequences float back into his vision. He sees spinning balls of light and a brilliant figure that appears to be an archangel. The figure of a hooded woman, or is it two, return to him. He is puzzled, yet at the same time oddly comforted by these images.

When the warden comes with armed guards to escort the prisoner to the quadrangle for his execution, he does not weaken or falter. Outside the prison gates, he hears the shouts of people calling his name, demanding his release. The sound follows him into the courtyard. There, he waits for the assembling of the firing squad. The wait is itself a form of mental torture. The young man does not look at the spot where so many of his friends and comrades have already died. He does not watch the soldiers walk in and set up in formation. Jan looks directly at a patch of dry grass in front of him and waits patiently. His thin, worn face is vacant and expressionless; his sharp eyes stare, fixed and unblinking. Suspended in the emptiness of the void, he is no longer aware of place or time.

The guards lead the prisoner to the post and secure him there. The soiled striped shirt and pants hung loosely about his body. He doesn't smell the clots of stale blood that cling to the dark cloth placed over his eyes. He doesn't hear the order given to the firing squad. But he feels the explosive, life-shattering pain in his chest and feels his body begin its crumbling fall to the ground.

What happens next is a sequence of events experienced in slow motion. First, Jan senses the presence of a woman. It is the same woman he saw the night before in his dreams. This time she shows her face. Murmuring soft and soothing words, she gathers his bleeding and broken body into her arms and presses it to her breast. Then she pulls his light-body upward and soars with him to a height above the ground from which they might see the courtyard. Jan sees his lifeless body and witnesses the final shot to the head. He watches as the guards take his corpse away.

Floating in the company of this magical woman, Jan finds himself hovering in mid-air outside

Barbara Paul-Emile

the prison. There he sees the full force and rage of the crowd. People are overturning cars, burning the flag of the country, and vowing vengeance against the officials. He sees men and women weeping impotently at a loss they cannot name. The heaviness of their grief is harder to bear than the shot which took his life.

As Jan glances at the calm countenance of the woman who has cradled him so tenderly, fragments of what he had considered his fantasies come floating back to him. I know this woman, he thinks. I know her well. He struggles to recall the circumstances of their meeting.

Suddenly, Jan experiences a quickening of his energies as he is drawn by a powerful magnetic vortex into a spiral opening before him. For a moment, he feels panic, and looks to his companion for assistance. She continues to hold him showing no sign of fear. Gratefully, he draws strength from the serenity of her presence. As he enters the swirling spiral, she releases him and he feels himself sucked into a tunnel where he floats towards a blinding light. The brightness at the end of the tunnel, the spinning motion of the vortex and speed with which he is carried through the spiral, all produce a sensation of dizziness and feelings of fatigue and exhaustion. By the time he reaches the end of the passage, Jan is weak and empty.

Although he feels no pain, there is a sense of unease for he has no idea where he is. The surrealistic experience he has undergone has all the elements of a wild dream. Jan tries to focus his vision and gain his *bearings. Is this death? he asks himself. Then, as though in response to his query, the haze that has blurred his vision begins to lift and figures to take shape. The first face he sees is that of a loving woman, this death-walker, who has come for him. He wonders whether she is an angel or a goddess. She must have sensed his thoughts for she motions him to be still and rest. How long he rests, he does not know. But he awakens to find himself on an elevated platform: a healing table.*

Jan looks about him and sees the faces of light-beings, so filled with high and loving vibrations that he is momentarily dazzled by their colors. A radiant entity, smiling as though in recognition, comes towards him and says, "Welcome, Jan. You have done well."

The words, the face, the woman ... Instantly all makes sense. Knowledge unfolds within him like the opening of the flower that blooms at evening. Jan, looking closely at the figure, says, smiling with gratitude and relief, "Satron, Light-Keeper ..."

Becka watched the scene with a sense of awe. She realized how privileged she was to witness Jan's crossing. She had sent her strength to him. She, too, had contributed energy to replenishing his auric field as he passed through the spiral. As the seer meditated on the implication of what she had seen, she felt an urgent tugging at her consciousness. The energy was Mosca's.

Becka finds herself with the African in the hot cane fields. He is not aware of her presence because he has not allowed himself to consciously access the energies of his alternate selves. Becka watches as he focuses his attention on his grueling work. The sweat courses down his face and his shirt sticks to his back.

He has told no one of his dreams, but all morning fragments of images keep coming back into his mind. He keeps seeing strange-growing, twisted plants instead of the pale-colored cane wrapped in brown stalks. As he struggled to anchor his consciousness, Mosca wonders what he ate the night before. He knows many who have become sick and lost their minds through the intake of poisonous potions.

After weighing these possibilities, Mosca's random thoughts move to a more pleasurable subject. He wonders if he'd been dreaming of Sika. But then, I always dream of Sika, he laughs, bitterly. Snatches of remembered songs and harmonies drift in and out of his consciousness.

In this disturbed frame of mind, Mosca works all morning lost in reflection and speculation. At noontime he sits by himself thinking further about his crazy dreams. In his own land he would have had them interpreted for him by the elders, the griots. Here, he dare tell no one.

A friend, simply known as Tom, because the busha cannot be bothered to pronounce Oswego, his given name, comes to sit beside him and examines him closely. He asks if Mosca is troubled in some way, since he had eaten none of the meager rations provided by the master and has walked to the field by himself. Further, Oswego notices that his friend has no good words for anyone this morning. Mosca smiles good-naturedly, and says that all is as it is.

Still troubled, however, by the free-floating fantasies in his head, Mosca runs through the activities of the previous night with Oswego, to discover if anyone has fallen ill or suddenly become delusional. Further, he has Oswego confirm for him that he has not been drinking heavily the night before. Oswego lays all of his friend's fears to rest. He was as sober as a preacher the night before and no one has suddenly become ill.

Alcohol or subtle poisoning could not, then, be blamed for what is occurring in his head, Mosca decides. What is the answer? Lost in his private thoughts, he gives only partial attention while Oswego, always a lively fellow, tells him all the gossip of the day.

Mosca, though always amused by Oswego's stories, has little to say for himself. He has learned not to talk freely and not to acknowledge all he knows. For his part, Oswego is always talking about running away, even though he has been cautioned by Mosca about the dangers of a loose tongue. This time, Oswego shares his new plans with Mosca. The scheme is much more advanced and the arrangements more detailed. The day and time have been set for the escape. Again, Oswego asks Mosca if he would join him and his friends. Mosca smiles to himself and thinks: *"Do you think that I am fool enough to say yes, readily, to such a question?"*

Oswego continues to speak of the Maroons who live up in the mountains. *"They are African and they were free,"* he reminds Mosca. *"Their scouts come by night to help those who want to join their numbers."*

Runaways who join the Maroons take blood oaths and form a tight-knit, self-supporting community. Loyalty is the key element required for admission to a Maroon compound. Traitors are killed without ceremony.

The strength of the settlements has increased over time to such an extent that the English seldom send out soldiers to engage the defenders. The treacherous nature of the terrain and their efficient use of deadly ambushes has reduced the enthusiasm of the English commanders for search and capture raids. The Maroons have created an oasis of freedom within a slave society.

Again, Oswego puts the question to Mosca. The shrewd African grumbles a non-committal response and says nothing of consequence.

The work crew is sent back to the field at the end of the short respite. Mosca's machete, swift and sure, flashes through the cane. With no wasted motion, he cuts and piles, cuts and piles the stacks of cane. As he moves down the row, he mulls over what he has heard from Oswego. Figures from his dream, masked women and figures in shiny clothing drift in and out of *his consciousness. He tries unsuccessfully to push the thoughts out of his mind. This is madness, surely, he thinks.*

The muscles at the base of his spine grow heavy and Mosca feels the need to stretch his cramping back. He straightens up, throws back his head and looks up into the blue skies. There he sees a lone black hawk circling overhead. It circles, flies away, and circles again. Mosca watches it mesmerized. A hawk, a hawk ... there was something about a hawk in his dream. He continues to watch the bird, unaware that the busha has approached him on his horse with his whip. By the time he hears the snorting of the animal, it is too late. He feels the massive leather whip cut across his back. Mosca cries out and bends again to the cane; but this time he knows what the black bird means. For him it means freedom, freedom, freedom ...

Becka knows that in seven days Mosca will leave the plantation with Oswego. He will regain his freedom never to lose it again. As a Maroon, he will fight his way up through the ranks and become one of a triumvirate of chiefs that lead the fighters of the community in the cockpit country. Mosca will become known for his craftiness and his courage. His men will follow him willingly.

One moonless night, after his escape, Mosca's band raids a plantation to help those who sought freedom. A sizable group has risked their lives to

Barbara Paul-Emile

gather at Bamboo Bottom, the designated meeting place. Traveling in the dark, the party escorted by Maroon soldiers, arrives by daybreak at Accompong town, a Maroon stronghold high in the Blue Mountains.

During the screening of the recruits, Mosca notices a woman, tall and slender who stays well back in the crowd. Her face is turned away from him. Close by her side is a small male child. Mosca looks at her and his heart quickens. He rises from his seat and, with quick steps, walks towards her. As he approaches she turns and looks at him. Her beautiful face is covered in tears. It is Sika. The pale-skinned child at her side, looks at the tall man, whimpers, and clings closer to its mother's long skirts.

Silently, Mosca pulls her away from the crowd. Overcome by a mix of emotions - shock, pain, joy, grief- Sika cries out and embraces her husband. She begins to speak, but Mosca covers her lips with his callused hands and, holding her in his arms, calls out her name repeatedly, in gratitude and in disbelief: "Sika, Sika, Sika," amid his tears of joy and amazement.

Her name meant: precious jewel; his precious jewel. He had considered her lost to him. Gone ... he thought her dead. The gods had returned her to him. His hands shook as he studied her face and he wept openly and without shame as he pressed her against him calling out her name repeatedly. "Yes, my wife, my precious one, has been returned to me," Mosca told himself. *This time if we cannot live together, then we will die together."*

The couple spent long nights holding each other, touching, to affirm life and existence and talking about the lost years. Sika had been transported to the new world on a ship that had dropped its cargo both in the Carolinas and in the Bermudas. She, along with many others, had been taken to Jamaica where she was bought at auction with a view to increasing her master's slave population.

She worked as a cook in the great house and served the family. By night, as a bondswoman, she was compelled to serve her purchaser as sexual chattel. If she refused the master's advances, excuses were found to beat her. After the birth of her child, she was singled out for severe punishment by the mistress of the house. On her back she bears the scars.

Mosca listens calmly to her story. Then he tells her his own. In his telling, he shows little emotion for he too knows the cruelties of bondage. He shares with her, as he has with no one else, the agonies and the despair he has endured. He tells her of the special dream he had seven days before he made his bid for freedom. He tells her of the recurring figures in his visions. Mosca shares with his wife his belief that he would find her again as was foretold to him in a dream. Sika listens intently with amazement and with wonder.

Mosca tells her that he is not a superstitious man, but he feels the presence of others with him. A

Barbara Paul-Emile

goddess, he claims, showed him that the hawk was his emblem. He should be free, as the hawk is free. Together, they weep over family and friends lost on the long march and on the death- ships on their sea journey. They pledge themselves to keep and honor their freedom and to reverence the hawk, the swift, sleek bird, and recognize it as their guardian entity. Oswego makes a drawing of a hawk with wings outstretched, to be hung over the entrance to the couple's dwelling.

Mosca and Sika also reminisce about earlier times when they lived in their home village. They remember the old ways and all that will never be again. But before memories lead to dejection and despair, they agree to lay all regrets aside and rejoice in their good fortune, for they who have seen so much human suffering - separation, brutality, cruelties of all kinds, torture and death - count themselves unduly blessed to be together. In later years, the couple will add two more children to their family.

Sika's son born in slavery, accepts Mosca as father and becomes his faithful lieutenant. He listens to the counsel of his adopted father and learns his way of life. Mosca will not catch runaway slaves in return for treaties with the English. Neither will he nor Nanny, the female chief, barter their peoples' freedom for bribes and gifts. Death, he teaches his children, is not to be feared. He teaches, rather, that hardship in freedom is better than an easy servitude.

In Becka's final vision of Mosca, she sees him seated on a rock, hidden but with a full view of the main passes to the compound, taking his turn on the nightwatch, guarding the settlement. The air is fragrant with wild flowers and there is a full moon overhead. Nightwalker watches as the sentry sharpens his senses, attuning them to the slightest movement of wild creatures. She watches as he allows his consciousness to wander between the worlds, assured that he will be called back into body, immediately, if needed. As Becka bade good-bye to her good friend, brother and multidimensional self, she knows that courage, steadfastness and resourcefulness, all elements associated with his energy, will nourish and sustain her. Yes, she is Mosca.

Stefan's signal vibration was still weaker than the others, but that did not prevent Becka from hearing and responding to it.

The shaman enters the sea-merchant's house as he is taking his breakfast after awakening from a deep sleep. He has lain in bed longer than usual because he is troubled by the terrible dreams he'd had. Murielle, his wife, has barely started her morning toilet before her husband begins to regale her with half remembered dream-fragments that drift into his head. She listens for a while and, appalled by what she hears, asks him plainly how much wine he has drunk before going to bed. He was known to over indulge and then to play the innocent. Next, she cautions him about the general state of his health.

Stefan denies all charges of over-indulgence and declares that he only had his nightly two or maybe three glasses of wine with dinner. Murielle, knowing that he denies all when it pleases him, does not believe his declaration. She has known him to drink much more than he should and, of course, lie about it without shame or guilt. Murielle dismisses his dreams as nightmares resulting from his wicked ways.

Stefan, for his part, knows these visions are no nightmares. They are true and they are real. He saw incredible figures and they spoke to him. A pale and sickly young man and a beautiful woman, who looked like no other woman he had ever seen, had argued with him and made him feel at fault over some issue. He had been afraid of the woman, he remembered that.

There had been many other figures, but he cannot recall them clearly. Staring intently at the armoire across the room, Stefan suddenly remembers that there had been a man dressed all in lights, like a character out of a nativity play. He had felt close to this impressive figure but he could not see his face. There had been flashing lights and glass-covered walls. All these things had taken place in a peculiar setting with strange rope-like trees and plants. Ah, yes, he recalls, he had flown with others, among them an African, who like him were specks of light.

Murielle listens to Stefan's fantastical tale with as much patience as she can muster. But as the scenes become more and more hallucinatory, delusional and bizarre, she realizes that besides being selfish and difficult to live with, her husband is now losing his mind. The good wife offers sound common sense advice: she suggests that her husband be bled to rid his body of noxious humors. Further, Murielle makes Stefan promise never to relate these strange and fanciful encounters in front of the children as neither the priest nor the bishop would approve.

The merchant goes to work as usual at the shipping house, but not before letting his wife know, with some passion, that he is displeased with her general response and will ignore all her admonitions. Arriving at the dock, Stefan watches the outfitting of a cargo ship. After his last bad business venture, he has been more careful about the vessels in which he invests. He has no desire to lose any more funds. Just before noon, his friend Jacques de Boucher approaches him with information about a ship ready to set sail for the west coast of Africa. It is an English ship, for it is the English who now control the slave trade. With their large fleet, they have challenged and defeated the Dutch, the Spanish and the French. De Boucher reminds Stefan that the ships are fast and safe and while the initial investment might be steep, the return will be sure and very profitable. The slave merchant listens with interest, but says he wants time to think about the proposition.

After de Boucher leaves, Stefan thinks about his investments over the years. There were some tricky times, but by and large, he has done well. Some others might consider him greedy and grasping, but he does not consider himself as such. He has made safe investments. Sometimes the risks were higher than other times, that was all. But this offer. What should he do about it? He sits quietly looking out to sea.

Several thought-impulses come to him. The most interesting one suggests that it is time to be done with this business. Although he supports it publicly, it is, after all, human flesh he deals in. It is a nasty business, not really respectable. For a moment these strange thoughts surprise him. Then Stefan remembers that not all bishops or archbishops condemn the trade, neither did all parsons. Still, his wife had objections. Maybe he should listen to her. But Murielle is a difficult woman, he thinks. She spends much more than she should on the household accounts and other trivial expenditures and then complains about the source of his income. She knows nothing of business. He decides to discount her views.

Inexplicably, images from last night's dreams again flash into his awareness. There are more visions of spinning balls of light and swimming dust particles. Stefan recalls that the beautiful and terrifying woman had not liked his trade either. But what business is it of hers? What business is it of anyone? It is only his business. This proposition is a business decision, merely a business decision.

Stefan looks out across the rolling waves. Soon his inner rhythms fall in with the motion of the water and a light trance settles over him. An image of the

*black man whom he had met in his dreams again
enters his consciousness. He is tall. His body,
hardened by physical work, has an odd familiarity
about it. He has an object in his hand ... He stands
with other people ... He ... Stefan sits perfectly still so
as to hold the thread of the thought-forms and not lose
the connection...*

*It is no use. The cawing of sea gulls wakes him
from his rêveries and the memory-links disappear.
Stefan shakes his head as though to clear it. He has a
strong feeling that something important happened last
night. If only he knew what it was ...*

Becka watched Stefan and wondered what she
could do to help him. She chuckled to herself when she
thought of what the unreconstructed Mosca would
have said about her dilemma. Nevertheless, she knew
that the demons with which the merchant wrestled
were real. She felt his confusion and understood the
struggle, taking place within him. Stefan was that part
of the self that, feeling disconnected from the whole,
had not developed feelings or concern for others. It
was his isolation that was his abyss.

As the shaman thought about connectedness,
a dream-figure dressed in old mariner's clothing
approached Stefan.

*The sailor's features appear thin and drawn.
His days before the mast have been hard and his limbs
are shriveled and thin. He sits down next to Stefan*

Barbara Paul-Emile

who, shifting uneasily in his seat, rises up and walks tentatively towards the window. Becka realizes that although Stefan is not consciously aware of the presence of the entity, he has registered its presence.

The merchant paces back and forth in front of the window, looking out at the comings and goings on the dock. Abruptly, he stops, turns and says aloud, "I am tired of the sea. It is too risky a business. At my age, I should be doing something else. The voyages take too long and the returns are not as sure as they used to be." Stefan listens to himself and growls under his breath.

He closes his eyes and rubs his chin, adding, "No. I will not invest with de Boucher. I am finished." With those remarks he walks to the desk, takes paper and quill and begins to write.

Stefan calls the office boy, hands him a scribbled note and says, "Deliver this to M. de Boucher."

As the messenger reaches the door, Stefan hears himself say, "Wait, boy, maybe I should explain my reasons." Then he stops himself and says, "No. Go on."

Becka was given to know that de Boucher, and others, would try to bring Stefan back into the trade. His leaving so abruptly would make them feel uncomfortable. If his business had not gone well, they would have understood and would glory in their own successes. But Stefan's departure, while in a good position to make profits, would give the wrong impression. It could potentially lead the misguided to raise moral and ethical questions. All effort would be made to get him back into the business.

Becka wondered what Stefan would do the next time he was approached. She sensed that he was investigating new ventures in the world of business. He was attuned to the shift in markets. Would he listen to his alternate selves and hold his own? Or would he vacillate, tune out, and be persuaded that "business was business." Right now, Stefan was calling in higher vibrational fields and was finding the internal strength to lift himself. He was listening and he was acting. His life will not be lost to the impulse to follow the herd.

The seer remembered the words of the HeartSong: Separate though together. In oneness, yet apart.

Stefan had begun to face his dragons. The terrain would be rough and the outcome unpredictable. Many difficult battles would lie ahead. The seer sent him clarity, courage and a blast of her heart-energy as she gradually withdrew from his presence.

The dreamwalker finds herself once again in Joe-Joe's room. As she settles into her body, she hears the birds welcoming the dawn as night begins its retreat before the coming of the day. The soft light of morning enters the room and all familiar objects take on a rose-colored glow.

Becka glances about her. All seems the same,

yet all is different. She sees the same cricket bat and ball in the corner, with which Joe-Joe will soon be playing. She sees his clothes hanging in the make-shift closet. The shaman smiles to herself, for these items which seemed so sad and forlorn before are now symbols of joy, of resurrection and of life. The child moves in the bed, opens his eyes, looks at her and called for his mother. Then he drifts off again to sleep. Becka tucks the sheets around him in gesture of loving comfort. "The child will live," she says to herself. "This child will live." A song honoring life and nature flows into her consciousness:

> *All growing things*
> *Salute the goddess*
>
> *All life restored*
> *Spring from her depths*
>
> *With her loving arms*
> *She cradles and makes whole*
>
> *With her great love*
> *She honors and bestows*
> *Life is a mysterious gift*
>
> *Give thanks for life!*
> *Give thanks for life!*

Becka's guides began to fade from view, but

not before she thanked them for their care and guardianship. Switching her focus to Joe-Joe lying peacefully in his bed she wondered about his dreams. What will he remember? The amnesic effect of earth's atmosphere would wipe away most of his knowledge. His consciousness would retain only fragments of what had taken place and even these would be filtered and translated into forms and images the rational mind could interpret and understand.

The obeah woman continued to monitor the child lying in the bed. His breathing was growing stronger. He coughed a few times to clear his lungs, and began to move his arms and legs. She touched his forehead. The fever was gone. His skin had lost its dry and ashy look and felt soft and cool to the touch. Becka marveled at the speed at which his body was recovering. Great bands of love went out from her to this child, for in her search for his life, she had found her own.

Chapter Eighteen

The Web

$\mathscr{B}$ecka, dreamwalker, moved quietly about the room and stretched her stiff limbs. She should feel tired, but did not. Instead, she felt exhilarated and alert. The hour was still early, but she knew that the household would soon be waking up. Traffic had increased on the road and Sojey would be arriving. Mirri, released from the influence of the sleeping potion, had begun to stir. Becka took a towel and decided to refresh herself by splashing water on her face.

Before she could fetch the water, she heard the sound of an automobile engine at the gate. Quickly, she went to the door and opened it. Sojey stood before her. The man looked haggard, tired, frightened.

"How is my boy?" he demanded. "How is he?"

Before she could answer, he pushed past her and entered the house. With long strides, he was at his son's bedside. He knelt and looked closely at Joe-Joe.

The shaman regarded him compassionately.

She said, "The child will live. He will live to be a man. He has made it through the night."

With tears streaming down his face, Sojey said, "I feared the worst. I tried to get here sooner, but could not. There was no conveyance. The mail van broke down. How is Mirri?"

He spoke but his eyes never left Joe-Joe's face. There was silence. He placed his hand on the child's face and said, "Poor Juppy, poor Juppy. And your Pappy wasn't even here to help you. ..."

There was a sound in the room and Becka turned to see Mirri behind her. She had been awakened by the voices. She looked dazed and astonished to know that she had slept all night. Sojey rose and went to embrace her. She quickly released herself and rushed to her child's side. She saw the changes immediately. The fever was gone. So was the stiffness, the frailty, the shallow breathing. He had made it through. She looked at Becka and then at Sojey, a smile breaking on her lips. Her eyes filled with tears. Sojey said proudly, "He gone live. He gone live."

Both parents, overwhelmed with joy, looked at the dreamwalker. Mirri said, "How we going to pay you for saving our boy? I knew you would heal him. I knew it. God showed it to me."

Before Sojey could speak, there was another knock at the door. It was Edna, Mirri's neighbor. She asked apprehensively, "How is Joe-Joe?" She did not ask if he had made it through the night, but everyone knew what she meant.

It was Sojey who answered, with much bravado and a confident I-told-you-so smile, "Nothing to worry about, man. The boy is fine. He gone live. Fever broken and everything, man."

His seemingly flippant remarks did not fool Edna for the signs of worry, fear, strain and exhaustion were written all over him.

Without responding, Edna went quickly to the child's bed. It was obvious that Joe-Joe was, indeed, much better. Compared to how the child looked the night before, he had made a miraculous recovery. She looked at both parents and said, "Thank God Almighty," and looking at Becka, she said, "And thank Becka." Emotion overcame her and she also wept.

Becka watched silently, as the sobbing women hugged each other. Sojey tried to comfort them with unsteady hands. The sobs were deep and wrenching but the seer knew that this release was necessary. Sometimes joy and pain had the same manifestation. The strain had been great. The release would be great also.

To create needed activity, Becka said, "Joe-Joe will want something to eat when he comes 'round. How about some clear chicken broth?"

She knew that this would keep everyone busy, because if the store was out of frozen chicken, as it frequently was, a live fowl would have to be caught and range-raised chickens are as lively and as speedy as they are tasty. Catching one would take time and ingenuity.

Mirri gained control of herself and answered, quickly, "Yes, of course. Where is Sam? He has to go to the store for me."

Early though it was, someone had to wake up Mr. Chin, the shopkeeper, and tell him that Joe-Joe was better and needed chicken for broth. Samuel answered the summons instantly, which told everyone that he has been outside the door listening all along. His round face was bright with smiles and joy rippled through his body. He took the money from Mirri's hand and ran to knock on the shopkeeper's door.

Mirri heard movement in Joe-Joe's room and ran back to the bed before Becka could get there. Her son had opened his eyes and was calling for water. Sojey ran to the small ice-box for cold water.

Becka said, "No. Take cool water from one of the jars."

As Joe-Joe looked around the room, his mother fetched extra pillows to prop him up. He looked thin and feeble but he was alive. He sipped some of the water and lay back exhausted. Becka monitored Joe-Joe's responses carefully and gave instructions regarding his care. She gave herbs for his tea and ointments for his body; all of which Mirri placed carefully in her cupboard.

Before the shaman left Joe-Joe's room, she heard him whisper, "Mother Becka, Mother Becka, I had … long dream … plenty people in it. Santa Claus… nice to me … gave presents."

Joe-Joe paused gathered his strength and continued, "Hear music ... feel like Christmas. I was like superman ... fly."

His talking seemed to weaken him so much that Becka said comfortingly, "Yes, yes, I know. I know. I was there."

The child explained, "No ... no ... talking about the dream."

Becka sighed and said, taking his correction, "Yes, I mean I understand. We will talk about this when you are better. Now you must rest."

But the child would not be silenced, too eager to share his experience: "Mother Becka, trees ...trees ... strange looking. And plants too ... I wasn't really scared." Making the last statement clearly gave him a sense of relief.

Becka sat down on the chair next to the bed and, looking lovingly at the child, said, "Joe-Joe you are a very brave little boy. Your parents are lucky to have you. You will grow into a fine man. Your dream was a wonderful dream. Now go to sleep and remember that all of us love you."

No sooner had Becka finished speaking, than voices drifted in from outside the room. She could hear Mirri saying firmly, "Not now, man. It isn't time for that yet."

Sojey responded stubbornly, "But I got it for him and I must show it to him."

The happy father came into the room with a large box in his hand. He opened it on the floor and smiling sheepishly, took out a beautiful, used guitar. He said, "A man was selling it and I bought it. I bought it for Juppy." Looking at Joe, he knelt and presented it.

The child's eyes glistened at the sight of the instrument. He struggled to raise himself but fell back. His father placed his gift on the bed. Joe-Joe ran his hands over the smooth wood and smiled. He continued to stroke the instrument intermittently and finally just rested his hand on it. Both Becka and Sojey could see him drifting off to sleep. Sojey made a motion as though to move the guitar, but the child's fingers were curled around it. Becka smiled and signaled him to leave it on the bed. Both drew the curtain to the room and left silently.

Mirri, noticing that her husband and Becka left Joe-Joe's room without the guitar, and curious about what had taken place there, peeked in at Joe. He had pulled the guitar close to himself and was hugging it. Laughing to herself, she arranged his pillows being careful not to disturb his new treasure. As Mirri looked around the room, she tried to remember how she felt last night when death was the stalker. Nothing seemed real. Maybe it had all been a dream, she thought. Today, her main concern was to restore her son to health.

Mirri's thoughts shifted to Becka. She was widely known as a healer who had succeeded where all else had failed. Once again, she had proved herself. Soon Joe-Joe's story would be the talk of the community. And rightly so. She had overheard a part

Barbara Paul-Emile

of the conversation between Joe-Joe and the shaman, and was touched by the deeply loving way the seer spoke to her son. She sensed a bond between them. Both she and Sojey knew that they were in Becka's debt and must find a way to show their gratitude.

Becka was calling for her walking stick and shoes and declaring that it was time for her to go, for the sun would soon be above the horizon. Mirri invited her to share breakfast with them. Known for her hospitality, Mirri had taken the best her cupboard had to offer. She was ready to serve coffee, tea, hard-dough bread, codfish, ackee, bammies, eggs, or anything Becka wanted. The seer agreed to a cup of tea and warm bammies.

As they ate together, Mirri thanked Becka for allowing her a night's sleep. But the mother felt ashamed and embarrassed, for she had left Becka alone all night. At this, Becka laughed and said that if she hadn't slept, there would have been two patients. Both laughed at the picture that would make.

Sojey shared with them his night's adventures: how he came to hear of Joe-Joe's turn for the worse, how he searched for a ride home and how strong his faith was during all that time. Becka felt he was rehearsing the tale that he would repeat, to friends and strangers alike, many times over in the Village Square, until the fear and pain surrounding the event had passed.

As Mirri poured fresh tea from the steaming pot, Becka asked her about her family. From Sojey's remarks, Becka surmised that there had been problems with the in-laws. Mirri's family had not wanted her to live so far away from home. In fact, they were hoping that Sojey would move up into the hills where they were. Sojey had flatly refused, and had taken his wife and left.

Visits had not been happy affairs. But Mirri managed to remain close to her family and had a loving relationship with them. Her old father was still living. From time to time, he sent provisions for the household. Sojey interpreted this gesture to mean that the old man doubted his ability to take care of his wife and son. He was wrong, of course, but, nevertheless, life had not been easy for him and he was touchy where money was concerned.

Sojey's family, as she well knew, had always been in what could, euphemistically, be called the retail business. They bought and sold food-stuff. Rumor had it that Sojey's father did not always buy - not strictly anyway! Neighbors had complained continually about missing produce. But let bygones be bygones. Sojey's brothers considered themselves respectable members of society now. Becka sipped her tea meditatively.

Her glance took in the home Mirri and Sojey had made. The rooms were small but clean and orderly. The most space was allotted to the main living area, which served for both reception and dining purposes. Tables, chairs, and a cabinet were carefully arranged against the wall to give the illusion of space.

Barbara Paul-Emile

The large mahogany table, the focal point of the room, was an excellent example of the maker's woodcraft. Becka had always admired the workmanship of this piece for its heavy-hewn appearance and the intricacy of its design. Sojey had given it to Mirri as his wedding gift.

The curtains at the windows were elaborately embroidered, as were the stack of tablecloths Mirri kept folded neatly in the cabinet drawers. Embroidery was her specialty. She made extra money by doing piece-work for the villagers.

The walls were covered with colorful pages taken from magazines showing nature scenes and attractive advertisements. New pages replaced the old as the paper aged. There were two photographs on the side table. One was a baby picture of Joe-Joe in his christening dress; the other showed Mirri and Sojey on their wedding at the Burchell Baptist church.

The shaman felt led to ask about Mirri's ancestors. Before Mirri could answer, Sojey jumped in and explained that Mirri's entire family, on both sides, were descended from Maroon fighters. Then, he added laughingly, with only a hint of malice, they are still as proud and as stubborn. Sojey was himself a Caribbean mix of African, Scotch, Irish, and probably more besides.

Showing great respect for her ancestry, Mirri said, "I will tell you the story of my family one day. Our great ancestor kept his African name and never changed it. He never accepted an English name.

Becka smiled and sipped more of her tea.

Mirri continued, "He was one of the fighters who negotiated land treaty with the English. He is remembered in history." Then she added proudly, "We have been written about by the Institute of Jamaica."

Sojey's looks indicated that, history or not history, he was not about to change his views about those old mountain people.

Mirri's voice trailed off ...

Becka was interested in the subject and wanted to know more, but she did not press. She allowed conversation to flow amiably and naturally. When, following Becka's directions, Mirri left the table to feed Joe-Joe his tea, Sojey became very serious and said, "Mother Becka, we cannot thank you enough for coming and caring for Joe-Joe. Mirri was alone and she didn't know what to do. You answered the call and came. From what I understand, things looked bad. I know you don't want praise. I know that. For you are a praying woman, but God use us to help each other. Now, Joe-Joe don't have a godmother and, frankly, I have never felt that he needed one. But Mirri and I have been talking ... We would like to ask you to be his godmother."

Becka smiled and was silent. Her thoughts flew off to the night's experiences ...

Sojey took her hand and said, "So what you say?"

Becka laughed and said, "I accept. You think I would refuse such an offer?"

Sojey let out a roar of laughter and the teacups rattled on the table. Mirri who had just returned from Joe-Joe's room told him to hush. But when she heard the news, she also laughed out loud with pleasure.

Becka looked in at her godson one more time before leaving and anointed his body with the mixture of herbs she was leaving behind with his mother. Both parents accompanied her to the door. The shaman, medicine bag in hand, headwrap freshly tied, walked to the gate. Who did she find waiting for her there? Samuel. He had already collected her walking stick.

Dressed in clean overalls over a finely pressed blue shirt, the young boy said, "If you want, I will walk home with you, Mother Becka."

Sojey looked at Becka, smiled and said, "Looks like you have a suitor. They start young these days, you know." Everyone laughed at little Samuel's discomfort.

Becka patted him on the head and handed him her bag. Looking at him, with humor and affection, the old seer said, "This suitor is accepted."

Amid much laughter, both figures set off down the road. Edna, waved from her kitchen window and told her son not to linger at Mother Becka's, but to return home promptly so that he wouldn't be late for school.

The seer and the young boy walked along in silence. Contentious cocks were crowing to awaken those who still doubted that morning had broken. Industrious chickens had already flown down from their roosts and were looking for food, anticipating a busy day. Shops were just opening up and small groups of workmen were on their way to their labors. Cars, buses and market trucks drove along noisily on their way to town.

As the couple drew close to Steely Hill, Becka said to her silent companion, "You are up early this morning. Do you always get up this early?" Samuel responded by saying that he slept fitfully last night. He kept thinking of Joe-Joe and wondering if he was going to get better. Becka, suddenly, realized that Samuel had not been allowed to see his friend this morning. Regretting the oversight, she took time to explain Joe's improved condition.

Samuel asked if Mother Becka was now Joe-Joe's godmother. The seer gave acknowledgment and added he might be seeing more of her now as a regular visitor to the Foleys. Both Becka and Sam were conversing amiably together when they noticed a car slowing as it approached them. It came to a stop, and two fashionably dressed women got out and came forward to greet the seer. One of them, Greta Perkins, she knew well, the other was a stranger to her. Greta introduced her cousin, Mel, who was visiting from the neighboring district of Malden.

After the usual courtesies, Becka explained that she could not stay to talk as long as she would wish, for Samuel had to get back to school. Greta inquired about Joe-Joe's health. Word had gone out that he was seriously sick. Becka said that he was recovering well

Barbara Paul-Emile

and would be up and about very soon.

Before the conversation ended, Greta said, "Becka, my cousin has not been in good health since she has been visiting me. Nothing she eats agrees with her. I am worried about her." Then she continued, laughingly, "I don't want her to refuse to visit me again because my food don't agree with her."

Becka looked closely at Mel as though sensing her vibration and scanning her field and then asked Sam to walk on up ahead, saying she would catch up with him. After the child had walked away, Becka laughed and said, "Mel, you are going to have a child. You must know that."

Mel looked at her in astonishment. She had taken every known precaution because she already had three grown boisterous children: all boys.

Becka looked at her again and said, "This time it will be a girl. And a pretty little missus too." Becka kissed both ladies and made her goodbyes.

As she walked away, she saw a vague outline on her inner screen and thought with considerable amusement, so you are on your way already, little one. Both Greta and Mel surprised into silence by the news, gazed in disbelief after the departing figure of the shaman.

Samuel was sitting on a stone waiting impatiently for Becka. He knew that she would not be able to catch him if he kept on walking. As Becka reached him, she said, "You know, Samuel, you are really a good boy. I am sorry to keep you waiting. I want to give you a present. What shall it be?"

Without hesitation and with great excitement, the boy answered, "A drum. A drum. I want to learn to play the drum. Marse Art says he will teach me, but first I must get a drum."

"Then a drum it is," Becka said.

"When will I get it? Do you have one at home?" Sam asked, running ahead and walking backwards so he could look at her.

"No, I don't have one at home, but you will get your drum, never fear," the shaman responded.

The rest of the journey went quickly, as Sam told her all the rhythms he meant to learn. He also sang for her some of the songs he knew, making the sound of the drum in the appropriate places with his voice. Becka marveled at his vocal dexterity and encouraged him in his dream to be the premiere drummer in the island.

The seer told him that the drum is the heartbeat of the Great Mother. Those who hear her rhythms and play them truly are beloved by her. The drum beats out the song of the heart that keeps us steady on our path. Its rhythms are essential to all music. It speaks to us in its own language and calls us. Those who hear the call must always answer. They must answer, "Yes, yes to life."

Samuel listened to her with rapt attention. At her house steps, Becka bade her friend and escort good-bye, but not before giving him slices of ginger bread and plantain tart to enjoy at recess. The child ran off happy. Before leaving the yard, he called to remind her that he would be back next week for his drum. Becka laughed and told him "to walk good," next week he would have his drum.

....

Alone on her verandah, the seer stands and looks out across the yard. The other houses in the compound are empty. Her relatives have already left for work. The rhythmic sound of women breaking stones for the paving of the road can be heard in the distance. Corey, her neighbor, is shouting at his father-in-law disputing the amount of money owed and promising to pay the debt. Everything is much as she remembered. Yet everything is changed.

Slowly, the seer walks across the yard to her favorite stone, sits down and breathes in the fresh morning air. Mornings, she thinks, are a time of birthings and beginnings, a time for affirmations. The pristine quality of the energy of this time is special and it, too, is sacred. Morning is a gift - a box of sweet and precious things, unopened. The energy of the dawn is soft and bright, shining with promises and possibilities. It calls everyone to begin again, to join with earth in affirming life.

The shaman offers honor to the spirits of the morning. She honors them for their work in awakening the chemical processes of the trees and plants that keep them rich and green. She honors them for reminding the animals of their life-giving instinctual patterns that assure them life. She honors them for nurturing all nature with the fresh moisture of the dew; for calling all living things to come forward into the day; and for the hope and faith placed in the heart of humans that make them believe that each day can be a new day, a special day, a better day.

> *Sweet, sweet morning Spirit,*
> *I call to honor you*
> *I call to sing you my song of beginnings,*
> *openings and birthings*
> *Hear me! Hear me! Sweet morning Spirit,*
> *Take me on your journey*
> *Propel me with your energy*
> *Let me feel your glory*
> *Shower me with your majesty*
> *Spirit, sweet Spirit,*
> *Glorious radiance of the morning*
> *Hear me!*

The sun is fully above the horizon; the day has been launched.

The powerful momentum of the genesis is almost complete. Morning, Becka thinks, is the shining engine that propels the day into being.

The seer sends out her energy signature and the responses come back swiftly from her multidimensional selves, *"We are here and all is well."*

The shaman's aura glows bright with the

acknowledgment of connectedness and she transmits love-streams in confirmation. Imperceptibly, she begins to sense the glorious presence of the Keeper and opens her heart-center to be nourished.

The plants, trees, flowers and all living things are connected, Becka says to herself, as are all the peoples of the earth throughout time. The shaman allows the thought to reverberate through her being as she leans her back against the stone, the skeleton of the Great Mother, and puffs slowly on her pipe. The healing properties of the stone - hard, cold and smooth - anchor her energies and send them deep into the earth.

The beams of the morning sun, refracted by the glistening leaves of the fruit trees, spread their golden patterns in geometric forms around her. The nightwalker closes her eyes, centers her consciousness, and frees her spirit. She feels it sing out of her body and with it she rises into the higher realms. There she sees displayed before her, in its glorious resplendence, traces of the infinite web of life.

Time gone, past
Yet present and to come;

Time held like
A shiny skein of thread
Winding through corridors unknown
Pressing limits, fearless and alone;

Intrepid heroes
Follow inner calls
Journey out
To lands fantastical;

Return again to say
We are but one!
We are but one!

Barbara Paul-Emile

Epilogue

$\mathcal{S}$eated comfortably in Mirri's house, Becka didn't realize that she had dozed off until she heard her friend's voice calling to the neighbor, Edna, enquiring, nervously, if the shaman had arrived. Hearing that she had, Mirri's footsteps quickened as she approached the house. Worried that she might appear a poor hostess, Mirri began calling out her greeting even before opening the door. She found her visitor seated snugly in her best chair with a teacup at her elbow.

Mirri smiled her approval and asked: "How are you, Miss Becka? I'm sorry, Ma'am, that I'm so late. The Post Office is getting worse every day. One of my letters gone to Mr. Mackie, down the road. In fact, everybody is getting other people's letters. If you send messengers to the post you don't know what they'll get. Post Mistress can't see like she used to and she won't get glasses. Did you just come, Ma'am?" she asked solicitously.

Becka laughed at the business of the post and, putting Mirri at ease, said agreeably, "I relish the chance to take a little rêverie. You look tired, daughter. Let us go into the backyard and sip some of your famous sour-sop juice."

Relieved that Becka looked rested and in good humor, Mirri put down her parcel and, taking the juice pitcher with tumblers, proceeded out the back door to sit down with her guest in the shade of the large mango tree. Leaves fluttered lazily overhead, as the wind gently made its presence felt. Chickens scampered about the yard, yet there was relative peace as the children were in school and Edna's dog was taking its mid-day nap.

The women laughed and talked together about the happenings in the village, the high cost of farm produce, the political figures running for office and the increasing number of visitors to the island. Mirri remarked that everywhere she looked there was new construction for hotels going up. Now, whenever she went into town she saw more and more tourists. She glanced at Becka, enquiringly, expecting her to explain the implication of the phenomenon. There was silence. The wind had died down and the humid heat of the afternoon pressed in upon them moistening their skin.

The seer turned inward contemplating the changes. She took another sip of the thick, sweet, sour-sop juice and, looking out across the yard, watched the heat shimmer as it danced over the surface of the earth, leaving behind a delicate, gossamer, transparent glaze.

Turning to Mirri she said, thoughtfully, "Child, we all make our journeys. Our visitors believe that they are traveling back in time to an island fantasy, a dream-world, the Eden of life. They journey here for the sun and the sea, hoping to replenish themselves in order to find what they've lost. They hardly know that we're here. But hear me, Mirri, the important journey that people should take they often put off. Our guests have too much of some things and too little of some other things."

Mirri laughed at Becka's perspective, for she felt that these sun-tanned visitors with money and leisure had all of whatever there was to be had in the world ... and the best of it too. But she knew better than to argue with Mother Becka, for the shaman was not always easily understood. She had her own sense of things and did not always speak of this world.

Becka enquired about Sojey and Joe-Joe. Mirri said all was well with the family but added, wistfully, that her son was taking too long to decide what he wanted for his life's work. First, he wanted civil service and now he is playing in a band with a bunch of other do-nothings. Tomorrow, it will be something else. The only thing he could be counted on to do was to enjoy himself. Mirri sighed and threw up her hands. If only he would listen to his father and get a good job in one of those new hotels. He could have a secure future because he would probably be put in charge of some important business function.

The shaman chuckled and said, "Let the boy be, Mother Mirri. You know the saying: 'Cloud come, but sun no set.' Joe-Joe will go round and round till he finds his way."

Mirri could not read the shaman's mind but her own thoughts flashed back to that particular and fateful night that had bonded them together. She felt a wave of emotional memory move through her body. Slowly, she leaned forward, poured more juice into Becka's glass and straightened the cushion at her back.

As the earth spun away from the sun, Edna's dog roused itself to welcome the afternoon and the laughter of children coming from school could be heard down the road. Becka asked for her scarf and walking stick, made her good-byes, and set off on her journey home. She had promised to make a stop at Moddie's house at the bottom of Steely Hill to hear the latest in a string of unsettling developments that seem to take place with dependable regularity, disturbing the delicate peace of that rambunctious and contentious family. Becka speculated that if she managed to extricate herself quickly enough from Moddie's fiery condemnation of her stubborn, wayward husband and her headstrong children, she might have time to pay a little visit to the Post Mistress before arriving home.

The seer glanced about her as she moved purposefully down the rocky incline. Twilight was approaching and the soft light of evening cast a magical sheen on the craggy hillside. The rhythmic tapping of her walking stick resulted in sudden furtive movements and rustling in the tall grass. The wild creatures were making their way home, Becka thought. Through the grace of the Great Mother, they had

Barbara Paul-Emile

survived another day. They also play their part in the great mystery that is life.

In the distance, the shaman heard the gurgling of Gully Springs as it flowed out from secret places in the earth to be embraced by its shallow, walled enclosure. At evening, the sound of the water rose above the stillness and was carried across the hillside. No voices could be heard now. The pool enclosure was quiet. But during the day, it was a meeting place, full of sound, color and motion - women washing, talking, laughing, swapping stories, fetching water to bring home, cautioning children wading in the pool, or watching the silver flow fill cupped hands and pour out between their fingers.

Becka knew that this was her community, her place, her home, and with that thought she drew in the sweet, delicate scent of the wild field-flowers, merged her consciousness with the sound of the water, and became one with her world, recalling Mother Moro's voice:

> *The times are fast changing ...*
> *While others break,*
> *You mend and hold your form;*
> *While others spin and eddy,*
> *Grasping at the flotsam on the bank,*
> *You flow forth like a river,*
> *Rich and steady in your currents;*
>
> *Spirit-energies flow through you;*

Spirit-strength sustains you;
The heart-flow of the Goddess
Steadies your rhythms;

Steady now, steady now;
Do you hear the call of the water
Flowing ceaselessly through time?

Do you hear it tell you
All is pantomime?
Life turns in endless rotation,
Streams to unfathomable oceans
Ever changing, ever returning,
Life!

Barbara Paul-Emile

About the Author

 **Barbara Paul-Emile's** cultural roots lie in the Caribbean. Her fiction, set in Jamaica and inspired by the rich mystical heritage of island culture, has appeared in American and Canadian journals. Her voice in Caribbean literature is an original one with strong cross-cultural appeal. Using language rich in lyricism and mythic symbolism, she captures the cadence of West Indian life and the magical interplay between the physical and non-physical worlds traversed by the Seer in serving the needs of the villagers.

Barbara Paul-Emile, Professor of English and Maurice E. Goldman Distinguished Professor of Arts and Sciences, holds a Ph.D. in English. Her work centers on 19th century English Literature, Myth and Caribbean literature. A member of the faculty at Bentley College, Waltham, MA, she was named Massachusetts Professor of the Year for 1995 by the Carnegie Foundation and the Council for the Advancement and Support of Education (CASE). She has published numerous articles on scholarly topics, but has remained true to her first love, creative writing. She is presently completing *Mosaic*, a

Collection of Caribbean Short Stories and a manuscript on the *The Spirit of the Warrior Woman.*

Email: BPAULEMILE@LNMTA.bentley.edu

6/05	DATE DUE		
AUG 0 1 2005			
NOV 2 3 2005			

Printed in the United States
26796LVS00002B/52

9 781887 472326